the
house
that christmas
made

ELIZABETH
BROMKE

ABOUT THIS SAGA

Welcome to Harbor Hills! Thank you for joining me in the final installment of this juicy suburban saga. Although *The House that Christmas Made* can stand on its own, you may want to consider reading books one through three in order to avoid spoilers for those stories and to get to know the characters.

Book one is *The House on Apple Hill Lane*.

Book two is *The House with the Blue Front Door*.

Book three is *The House Around the Corner*.

If you're ready to continue, here is a brief synopsis to remind you where the ladies are at the start of this story.

Quinn Whittle didn't wind up with O.C.D. for no good reason, and we're about to learn what that reason is. After settling in nicely on Apple Hill Lane, she hopes that the hardships of the past are behind her.

That is until her daughter Vivi makes a holiday threat that could undermine all of their mother-daughter progress.

Jude Banks is slowly growing closer with her neighbors, and even Dean Jericho doesn't seem so bad. But all of this is only possible because Jude has hidden her history so well. What if they learned the truth about Jude? Would they still accept her?

Annette Best and her family have moved into the *House Around the Corner*, and a new version of their business is blooming. Small-town, *small-scale* life is good, and Annette's friends are great, but the secrets of the past haunt the bubbly brunette. She must come clean about what she knows if she wants true peace in Crabtree Court.

Beverly Castle is doing well enough with her new writing assignment at the *Herald*, but she realizes that staying in the house where her daughter lived might be too hard. She has a decision to make about starting over or staying put.

The unnamed girl, now an *unnamed woman*, has learned of her grandmother's suspicious death, and it's up to her to help her grandfather move forward with the dark truth.

Happy reading!

Yours,
Elizabeth Bromke

For Jeanie, who embodies Annette's friendliness, Quinn's style, Beverly's heart, and Jude's depth. Thank you for being the glue on our very own "Apple Hill Lane."

PROLOGUE

The heady smell of seasoned turkey, brined and roasting to a sizzle, could not quell *the woman's* unease. She swayed in her grandfather's doorway as the other two faces within blurred together until they became one.

It took a moment for the woman to orient herself.

Here she was, standing on the front porch of 696 Apple Hill Lane, just as she had for the past several holidays now, ever since her grandmother had died.

She was supposed to go in and roast Thanksgiving dinner with her grandfather before dozing on the sofa. After, she'd tidy up. Then, she'd return home to Heirloom Island. To teaching and to her otherwise bland and lonely life.

That was the normal flow of things. But on this particular Thanksgiving Thursday, she'd arrived to find a *second* woman. A competitor. Although *what* was the competition? Was there any?

Most logically, this strange-but-beautiful lady was a relative. Yes. A relative.

Rifling through her memory, the woman conjured up her grandfather's full name to the best of her knowledge. Bernard Carlson. Middle name—to the woman—unknown. Nickname: Bernie. Or, in her case, Grandad.

Carl—that's what the strange lady inside had called Grandad upon opening the door.

Carl. A diminutive for his surname, Carlson? Odd.

Was there a sister? Grandad had several, yes. Sisters and brothers. But—they were shadows to her. Rumors.

The woman eyed both of the older people with great confusion before stowing the question of names away, deep in her brain.

"Kid," Grandad choked over the word, coughing and spewing for a dramatic moment. "I figured you weren't coming around."

"I always come around," she replied. For the past several years now, she'd arrived on every single significant holiday. Even some of the insignificant ones. Had dementia finally hit the wheezing old man?

No.

His already-ruddy cheeks flushed deeper, their pores darkening like sinkholes among the red blood-vessel spiderwebs on his cheeks. He groped for his walker and scootched to the side, offering the woman a better view of the *other* person.

The woman didn't step in and instead awaited a proper introduction.

Grandad cleared his throat awkwardly. "This is my granddaughter." He indicated her to his friend with a half-hearted sweep of his hand.

The woman tried for a smile, but all that came out was a grimace. "Hi," she grunted.

The other woman nodded, perhaps equally nervous. "Hello."

Without the exchange of names, a threatening silence had settled, forming a Bermuda Triangle between the trio.

The other woman licked her lips and took a tentative step forward. "I've heard so much about you," she said, her words sinking into the abyss of their uncomfortable meeting ground. Then, that unfamiliar, strange woman—who was probably ten years younger than Grandad and twice as beautiful as Nana—jutted out a delicate hand. "I'm Temperance. Temperance Temper. You can call me Tippy."

CHAPTER 1—JUDE

The world outside of Jude's parlor window was frozen in a perfect late-autumn tableau. Birches and oak trees reached for the frigid, white-blue morning sky like skeleton fingers toward Heaven.

In a stark contrast to those tall and lanky trees, vivid green still clung to the front lawn. Green that may or may not last. Oftentimes in Michigan, a warm spell followed by a jolting cold snap would damage the grass badly enough that, in years prior, Gene would spend a lazy Saturday reseeding, mulching, and accepting late-spring lemonades from Jude. Ever the perfect housewife.

That was Jude.

Back then.

But now, this year, the grass might well die, and

Jude wasn't quite sure if she'd have the oomph to fix it come the following summer. Of course, winter hadn't even hit yet. It was much too early to tell if *Jude* would even survive the winter herself, much less whether her front lawn would.

Presently, she took a long, slow pull of her coffee— a sweet holiday-flavored blend she'd dug out of the closet where she kept gifts to regift.

Dean Jericho sat no farther than eighteen inches away from Jude on her very own love seat. Together, they faced her front porch and the street, sipping their respective coffees. A generous spread of breakfast foods ornamented the square, wooden table that abutted their knees. Jude had put out two of each: croissants, blueberry muffins, sticky buns—all home-made. She'd added two bowls of cut-up fruit and two glasses of orange juice. Silverware and cloth napkins framed each of their appetizer plates. It had taken her, in all, just over three hours to prepare.

Dean set his coffee mug down and reached for a sticky bun. After taking a bite but *before* swallowing, he announced, "You're divorced." The statement bounced from his mouth like a flat basketball. Like he was pointing out the weather, dully. Lamely. Boringly.

Jude pitched her reply right back like the crack of a bat on a baseball. "Technically, my marriage was annulled."

Their get-together was meant to be another casual

attempt at a date, although Jude refused to acknowl-
edge such a label for any sort of meeting. And she had
only agreed at all because of how things were going in
the rest of her social life. Her friends were entrenched
in some hideous mystery. Even the school was
wrapped up in the age-old local missing woman case.
Jude had *no* interest in any of that. She wasn't one to
involve herself in gossip. And Dean seemed to be of
the same temperament. Not once had he mentioned
the body that the Bests had found *or* Temperance
Temper, the missing woman. So, for now at least, Jude
and Dean fit together well.

Dean pulled a suspicious frown. "Annulled?" A
chuckle followed. "Do people really get annulments in
this day and age?"

Jude recoiled with her coffee mug. "Catholics do."
She knit her eyebrows together. Wasn't he devout? And
if he wasn't...then what?

"I'm just plain old divorced," he replied, answering
a question she hadn't wanted to ask aloud.

"Oh." Jude took another sip. "How long ago was
that?" No, Jude wasn't up for gossip, but she *was* a red-
blooded woman. It wouldn't hurt her to know a little
about this Dean fellow's history.

"Peg and I quit each other twenty years ago. Just
about one year after our wedding."

"Oh." Jude pressed a hand to her chest. "One year?
That's..."

"Telling?" he finished her sentence for her. "Yeah. Never should have done it in the first place. Weren't a good couple."

"And it scared you off of marriage?" Jude slid her gaze back out the window, beyond which a light gust rustled loose pine needles free from their branches. Late droppers, Jude called them—the pine needles that ought to have fallen back in September and October but hung around until winter.

Dean gave her a funny look. "Scared off of marriage? Not to sound too macho, but there isn't much that scares me."

She lifted an eyebrow. "That might be the most macho thing I've heard." A little smile danced on her lips. "Then again, I don't consider myself one to scare easily, either."

"Then you won't be scared if I ask you something straight up." Dean put his plate and mug down and turned to her, his expression falling serious.

Jude tucked a strand of her silver hair behind an ear, willing herself to tolerate whatever it was he was about to say. Maybe he'd ask her why she got an annulment. Maybe he'd ask her about Gene. Maybe he'd ask her on a *real* date.

But Dean Jericho seemed entirely disinterested in Jude's romantic history...or future. Because instead, he simply scratched the back of his head and asked, "How did you know the Carlsons?"

CHAPTER 2—ANNETTE

Annette's husband had been acting strangely for at least a week now, and it was bad timing. Christmas was upon them, and they were in full rebrand mode with the business. New marketing campaigns. New clients. And a cramped house that doubled as an office.

Not only that, but then there was the active police investigation splayed across property lines.

Life was a mess, but it was *their* mess, so Annette figured she'd put up with Roman and his oddness. In the meantime, she had things to do.

And today, the main thing to do was her fourth interview with the police.

"No," Detective Grange assured her as they sat across from each other in the Harbor Hills Police Department interview room, "you're not a suspect."

"Then why are you interviewing me separately from Roman?" she put back to him. "And Elijah?"

"Because we have to do this thing right." Bill Grange was a Harbor Hills old-timer, having served on the force since he was fresh out of the police academy.

Annette took a long drink from her Styrofoam cup of coffee. "Fine. But I have a meeting at ten with a new client."

"You'll be out by then," he assured her, flipping pages in his notebook. "Okay, so the kids came to you and explained what they found. You assessed it and decided to keep it mum."

"Initially," Annette allowed. "But the next day I realized it might not be what I thought."

He gave her a hard look. "What do you mean?"

"I mean, I figured at first it was one of these backyard graves. There's a string of them in my new backyard on Dogwood, you know."

He nodded but stayed quiet.

"Well, I realized maybe it was something else. Then I remembered..." She hovered over the rest of her sentence, pondering whether to come out with it. Annette had a rule about honesty—if the truth could hurt someone, then shut up. She'd learned this from her older sister, and when they were younger, it felt good and moral. A righteous way to live, even. But now, sitting at a metal table with stale coffee in hand, she wondered if the truth could set her free.

But then, was Annette *not* free?

She was too far out of her element to even know.

"What?" Bill pressed. "What did you remember?"

"I remembered when we bought the house—" A thought seized her midsentence and she interrupted herself. "Bill, have they ID'd the body yet?"

He shook his head. "The labs in Saginaw and Detroit are backed up like crazy, but we *do* have a lead, and we pulled dental records. Waiting for those. If all else fails, we'll try for DNA."

Nodding, Annette realized if she *were* in trouble in any way, Bill probably wouldn't share such intimate details about the case with her.

Bill tried again. "You were saying you recalled something?" He took to his notebook. "What year would that have been, by the way?"

"Two thousand one. Or was it two thousand?" She shook her brown hair back and rolled her shoulders. "I just remembered that there *was* a disclosure."

"Oh." Bill fanned through his stack of papers and tugged loose what could only be a history of property information. Annette recognized the Best Realty logo across the top—her in-laws' business. "Was it *this*?" He slapped a singular page down and pointed with a stubby finger. Unlike Roman's hands, Bill's were dry and cracked, matching with the winter weather. Annette sometimes wondered what it said if a man had smooth hands. Was he a wimp? Effeminate? Was something wrong with him? Too soft? Then she thought about her own father's hands. Rougher than Bill's and dirtier, too. Hands that had touched a woman who was not Annette's mother. Hands that didn't deserve her.

She decided then and there that she'd take Roman's soft, faithful hands over rough, wandering ones. *Any* day.

Annette's eyes glanced over the paragraph the detective indicated.

She swallowed. "Yeah." Her eyes lifted to his. "But, *again*, I think those clauses pertain to almost every single house in Crabtree Court."

"And do you know why?" he asked, folding his hands together and leaning in.

"Because, like I said, that's what people *did*. There were no concerns over the water table back then. Big families took burials into their own hands. That's what Roman always said." But Annette wasn't even sure if it was true. In her upbringing, not once had she ever discovered a random backyard grave.

"It's exceptionally rare for a *true* family burial site to appear like this. And while, yes, we know about the Carlson cemetery on Dogwood, we don't know about this new one. The shallow grave in the *Becketts'* yard... isn't a proper burial by any stretch. No marker. No casket. Just inches down." He gave her a look. "Who did you buy this property from originally, Annette?"

She pursed her lips. "You've got the paperwork right here. You can see clear as day. The Tempers. First, we rented, then we purchased."

"And which Temper would that have been?"

"We never met them," she shot back. "Roman's parents coordinated the rental agreement *and* purchase. It's *exceptionally rare* for a home seller to meet his or her buyer." She liked using Bill's own words.

"But you rented first. Surely you sent your check to the Tempers, or they came around to fix something at some point." Bill scratched the top of his head.

"We sent the rent check in the mail, sure. Probably to a property manager." She snapped her fingers, awareness hitting her hard and breaking her anxiety. "That's right. It was a property manager. Again, though, even when we were renting, Roman's parents played middleman. They live in Birch Harbor like the Tempers. You should ask them."

"We did." Bill's mouth remained in a flat line. "They said it was Bernard Carlson who handled everything. That he was acting property manager on the Temper family's behalf. That the Tempers purchased the house from him, but he agreed to help them sort things out. All the paperwork, however, was signed by Bernard Carlson."

"None of the Tempers? I mean, did you call them?"

"All dead." Bill grimaced. "Their whole lot seems to be long gone."

"No wonder the missing persons case went stale," Annette murmured.

"Just because a missing person's family is out of the picture doesn't mean the mystery is solved."

Annette sighed. "But it means there's no one left to care whether it *gets* solved."

"Actually," Bill said, "in this case, there *is*."

CHAPTER 3—QUINN

Quinn and Vivi sat on the parlor floor surrounded by tubes of wrapping paper, gift bags, and the menagerie of presents they'd selected for people in their lives other than one another. A Hallmark Christmas movie played low on the TV, and a fire flickered in the background.

It was perfect. Things were perfect.

And yet...

Quinn's nerves weren't entirely settled for the season ahead. After wrapping these gifts, she'd have to set about serious Christmas shopping for Viv. And what did you get a teenage girl like Viviana? Quinn didn't know, and the not knowing vexed her terribly. How could a mother not know the perfect present for her own daughter? If she were a bad mother, that's how.

"Have you heard anything about the body yet?" Vivi asked her mother out of the blue.

Thinking for a moment, Quinn hesitated to indulge this particular interest of her daughter's. "Annette mentioned they are trying to make a positive ID. I guess it's not an immediate thing."

Vivi, blissfully unaware of the turmoil bubbling in her mom, grabbed a fistful of popcorn, shoveled it into her mouth, and spoke through chomps. "It's obvious who it is, though."

Quinn ran her scissors down a square of foil paper. "Well, yeah. It's probably a Carlson."

Vivi made a face. "No." She applied a piece of tape across overlapping sheets of wrapping paper, finishing her gift to her father—a nautical watch. "All of the Carlsons' burial records are in the files out there." She pointed with her chin toward the general vicinity of the garage.

"What do you mean *burial records*?" Quinn asked.

Vivi flicked her a glance, then crammed in another handful of popcorn before replying. "I thought you knew," she grumbled between chews.

"Don't talk with your mouth full," Quinn admonished. "And no. I don't know. What is it? Like, a log or something?"

Shrugging, Vivi answered, "Yeah. It's a book. I had

it sitting on the kitchen table the whole time we were doing our research project."

Quinn had been only vaguely interested in Vivi and Elijah's morbid search for the missing woman called Temperance. "Oh. I guess I didn't notice."

"Anyway, the Carlson family wrote down every single person they buried. The dates and names are all in the book, and they match every single grave in Eli's backyard. It's not like anyone is unaccounted for."

"Next door? As in the Becketts' yard?" Quinn meant Annette and Elijah's *old* house.

"No," Vivi corrected. "In the red cottage. Behind us. Eli's *new* house."

"Oh."

"So, then, what about the body? You're saying it's accounted for in the Carlson records, too?"

Vivi gave her mom a look of exasperation. "*No*," she replied wearily. "I'm saying it's *not*."

"Then how in the world do you know who it is?"

"Process of elimination. It's *elementary*, my dear mother. Come on."

A commercial gave way, returning programming to the movie they'd been watching and momentarily stealing Quinn's attention. She couldn't help but admire the set decorations of all these Christmas shows. Over-the-top greenery and dazzling ornaments. Quinn really needed to step up her game. She dragged her eyes back to Vivi, who was wrapping up the smartwatch she planned to give Elijah—something they'd argued over. It was too much, Quinn thought. Especially when they were tracking every single December dollar and had already spent nearly one hundred bones on Matt's watch. They were tracking every dollar, period, actually. But Vivi had won, arguing that Elijah was her best friend, boyfriend, neighbor, *and* the son of her mother's best friend. It was a fair argument.

When it came to whom the skeleton might belong, Quinn had just one other guess. "So, then, it has to be that girl, right?"

Vivi gave her an odd look. "What girl?"

"The girl that Beverly's mom was talking about."

Rolling her eyes, Vivi said, "It's got to be Temperance Temper. The *missing woman*. Hellooo."

"Oh, right." Quinn quickly recovered by nodding and folding the wrapping paper neatly up the sides of a box of chocolates meant for Jude.

They both paused their wrapping to watch the hero and heroine embrace on the screen, a flurry of snow descending over their green and red sweaters and perfect hair. When the next commercial came on, Vivi spoke again. "But what girl?"

"What do you mean?" Quinn asked, popping her own handful of popcorn into her mouth.

"What girl was Beverly's mom talking about?"

"That *girl*," Quinn replied smugly. "You know. When we were at Bertie's for brunch, she said there used to be a girl who came around here." *Here* had officially come to mean the storied house in which Quinn and Vivi lived. At first, it had felt awkward referring to the past events of their new home. Now, it felt normal.

"You don't think that was Temperance Temper she was talking about?"

Quinn rarely had the chance to be one step ahead of her gifted daughter, so she decided she may as well revel in any moment when she was. "No. Temperance Temper was a missing woman. That happened years later. The girl came around here in, like, the seventies? Eighties? Anyway, don't you think someone like Bertie Gillespie would have noticed if a missing woman was haunting Harbor Hills?"

A fire came to Vivi's eyes. "Then who was the girl?"

Quinn just shrugged. "Maybe she's in those files out there."

CHAPTER 4—THE WOMAN

St. Mary's Catholic School for Girls boasted little more than chalkboard-lined classrooms and ruler-wielding nuns. But ever since World War II, it *had* kept alive a fully-functioning mail room, complete with a part-time attendant—the parish custodian.

Even long after the war, St. Mary's strongly encouraged pen pals. The little wards proved avid correspondents, as did the faculty. After all, living on an island, even one off the shore of Lake Huron, afforded little outside communication apart from those rare inland field trips.

Of course, in the wintertime, there were *no* field trips. No ferry rides to Birch Harbor for a slice of pizza on Saturday night or a fish fry the next Friday. Wintertime on Heirloom Island, there was no departing the parish hall or the dorms or anything. Doing so, one would meet only with the treacherous lake ice on the north of the school and swells of boot-swallowing snow on the south.

Only two spaces afforded themselves as formal common areas for the students and faculty. The kitchen, which was usually taken by whomsoever woke up first and got dibs on baking for the day. And the parish hall, which the girls avoided like the plague if there wasn't Mass or Adoration or another Sacrament to be attended.

Then there was the mail room. An unexpectedly and notably large room, lined with dark-stained oak boxes. The small ones were reserved for students. The large ones for faculty members. At some point in the seventies—if the fabric was any indication—a kindly faculty member or family had donated a matching set of orange corduroy sofas. The only place for the sofas —apart from the rectory, which was already suitably furnished for the priest at that time—was the mail room. And that's how the mail room became something of a social hotspot for the girls of the school, and sometimes even the faculty.

This dated, wood-walled space was where the woman found herself that last Sunday before Christmas. The one after her visit to Grandad's house at 696 Apple Hill Lane.

The woman stood in the mail room in front of her

big oak postal box and stared at the two envelopes that had been slotted within.

One, a nondescript mass mailer.

The other, familiar. A token of her recent Thanksgiving visit, even. Of the other part of her life. Her life *outside* of St. Mary's.

That familiar second piece of mail with its ornate *T* stamped across the back flap. The woman didn't even bother to open it. She didn't bother to fully admire the Christmas stamp or the snowflakes that lined the bottom. It was a Christmas card. Plain and simple. It meant nothing to the woman. Not now. She pulled a pen from her handbag and scrawled three words across the front center of the envelope.

Return to sender.

CHAPTER 5—BEVERLY

Beverly had agreed that she'd join Darry for the Christmas Gala, but she'd made that agreement during the harvest party. When she was high on a surge of fleeting happiness. Sometime after, Beverly realized why some people swore by the adage that one should never make decisions when they were feeling particularly good or particularly bad.

Now it was December, and the gala was closing in. So, too, were Beverly's moving plans. Her goal was to be out of the house before Christmas, but that goal was quickly turning into a long shot. She hadn't listed the house. Hadn't found a house to buy. Hadn't even prequalified for a loan, which she'd need, considering the market. Then again, if she left for an even smaller town, or maybe to buy a manufactured home in the middle of the woods, she wouldn't need a loan.

Still, could Beverly really stand to spend the holidays even more isolated than she already was? This one would be the second Christmas without Kayla, but in a way, it felt like the first one without her. Without Tom, too. How could Beverly possibly enjoy the festivities at all, much less with a former flame? It was laughable. The very notion. So, too, was the notion that she spend December twenty-fifth in a hollow, lonesome trailer in the wilds of Michigan, however.

Therefore, here she was. On a perfectly chilly winter Saturday at the boutique on Main, with her mother, searching for something to wear. Inertia had brought her here. The one-step-in-front-of-another thing that was life after death.

It felt a lot like prom had, back in high school. Then, Beverly had wanted to go dress shopping with friends, but she hadn't had too many of those. So, instead, she had trudged along the same racks as stood in the shop now, her mother flitting over her shoulder, approving of dresses that Beverly hated, all the while disapproving of dresses Beverly would have killed to wear.

"What about this, Bev?" Now, her mother held up a fuzzy, red sweater, complete with darts.

"Darts." Beverly pointed at the added seam meant to allow for at least a modest breast. "I've never seen a sweater with darts, and I've certainly never *needed* one."

Her mom shrugged. "Are you going for a white Christmas look?"

"I'm not going for *anything*, Mom. And if I were, I'd be going for...socially acceptable."

"Socially acceptable has become a low bar. How about this?" Bertie swung around a green tunic with red lace trim dripping from the bottom hem like bloody icicles.

"Yeah. I could pair it with striped leggings and play an elf for the tree lighting." Beverly sighed. "I'll just wear something I have."

"No, you won't. You have nothing." Her mother started looking more furiously through the clearance rack, while Beverly turned to the display mannequin in the front box window. From the sleek, slender, pale-white form was draped an elegant, cranberry-red sweater dress. Nothing too clingy or too shapeless. Just, *nice*-looking. The form was styled with black leggings, chunky, red, knee-high boot socks, and warm, velvety black booties. A black cotton scarf was fashionably tied at the neck. On the faux woman's head sat a slouchy black beanie. Nothing about the *look* was particularly modern or particularly dated. Nor was it especially seasonable—in terms of a Christmas gala, at least. Of course, Beverly's only real point of reference was her mother, who planned to wear an ugly Christmas sweater, unironically.

Beverly reached for the handwritten price tag hanging from one sleeve. Her eyes bulged.

"Yes." Her mother's voice came up behind her. "You're getting it."

"It's not even that Christmas-y," Beverly protested.

"All the better. You can wear it for more than just the gala, right?"

"Mom. Look." Beverly flashed the tag, but her mother was already at the counter, exchanging words with the shop owner.

Not fifteen minutes later, the two Gillespie women were striding out into the cold day, a paper shopping bag in each of Beverly's hands.

Beverly had collected her mother from the B&B and needed to drop her back off, but the car ride suddenly seemed too short. "Want to come over?" she asked her mom on a whim.

"To your house?" Bertie slid her a sideways glance. "Why?"

"Gee, never mind."

"You never have me over, Bev. That's all I meant. I'd love to come. Maybe we can dress your tree. Have you put it up yet?"

"Actually, I could use your help, but not with the tree."

"Lights? Did you ever find that glass nativity set you lost last year?"

"It wasn't lost, Mom." Beverly didn't have the

energy to explain to her mother that she hadn't put the nativity set up last year just like she hadn't put up a tree or lights or anything at all. Heck, she hadn't even made her bed all last winter. And of all of her Christmas paraphernalia, the nativity set would go up last. It had been Kayla's favorite piece. It was also the piece that had linked the Castles to God, and Beverly was still pretty angry with Him. "I didn't take it out. And I'm not taking it out this year, either. I'm not putting up any decorations."

"You've got to put up a tree." Bertie stated it like a fact not a suggestion. Last year's tragedy was more digestible for Beverly's mom. This made sense. She'd also lost her husband. She'd lost her own mother and father. An elder brother. She *knew* loss. She understood it. She accepted it as part of life. She took her losses and gave them to that same God so she didn't have to carry the weight. And, as a result, Bertie's words and thoughts were lighter. Her life, happier.

Beverly wasn't like that. Her grip on the steering wheel tightened as she pulled onto Crabtree Court to head home. "I'm not putting up a tree. In fact, I'm packing it." She kept her gaze on the road and its subtle curve to the pit of the cul-de-sac. "I'm packing everything."

Her mother made a harumph. "You mean you took it out and changed your mind?" Her hand curled over Beverly's wrist. "Oh, Bev. It's hard. Sometimes, doing things that are normal make you feel more normal. You know what I heard someone say one time? *Fake it until you make it.* That really helped me because I realized I could just—"

"Mom." Beverly twisted her arm from her mother's loose grip. "I'm packing my whole house. I'm...I'm moving."

"Where? Why? Beverly, what are you *talking* about? That's *Kayla's* house. You're not going to leave her, surely." Bertie had worked herself into a fever pitch, and her painted nail cut through the warm car air, pointing directly at the beautiful, dying house with its newly painted blue door. With walls and windows encasing so much heartache. Beverly knew that if she stayed, even for Kayla's memory, that house wouldn't be her home. It'd be her tomb.

CHAPTER 6—JUDE

The date with Dean ended on a decidedly sour note. Sour because of his unromantic Q and A—which Jude all but ignored—and sour because she had to teach the next day, anyway. Finals were upon them, and Jude hadn't finished her poetry unit yet.

Now it was Monday, and a copy of "Stopping by Woods on a Snowy Evening" stretched from the top to the bottom of her podium. Hers was marked over in her own notes. The copies on each student's desk remained virginal.

Jude asked the class for an examination of the speaker.

"He's a creep," Vivi replied. "He's, like, trespassing on someone's property. Right?"

"Okay, fair," Jude replied, ever favoring her beautiful little neighbor. "But is the act of trespassing the central occasion in this poem?"

"I don't think so," Vivi replied.

A boy's hand shot up, and Jude called on him. "Why would the speaker be in this forest if he was totally unfamiliar with it? I think he isn't trespassing exactly."

"What's your point?" Jude asked.

"Maybe he knows the property owner. Or whoever owns the woods. Maybe they're friends."

"Again, though," Jude went on. "Is this poem about the speaker's relationship with the unnamed, unseen *other* character? Or is this poem about a different relationship?"

"It's about humanity's relationship to nature." This response came from Vivi and drew a sharp focus from the rest of the class, Jude included.

"How do you know?" she asked the girl.

"We've done, like, *four* other Frost poems. They're always about nature and how people make decisions when it comes to being in nature. 'The Road Not Taken.' 'Birches.'" Vivi probably could have spouted off ten others that the class had *not* studied. She was simply that sort of student. Bizarrely attuned to the finer aspects of her English education. "And I, like, *get* it."

"What do you mean you *get it*?" Jude prodded.

"It's like we—humans, I mean—sort of forget about where we came from. Where we're going. It's only logical that a sensitive person, like a poet, is maybe closer to nature. And the struggle is *so* real."

"Is Frost arguing that 'Stopping by Woods' is about the struggle to return to nature? To leave society and stay there, in the lovely, dark, and deep woods?" Jude felt the electricity of a great class discussion. And even though it was mostly Vivi and her talking back and forth, all eyes were on them. All ears. All brains. *On.*

Vivi replied melodically, "*That* and 'miles to go' before he sleeps."

And in Jude's head, she echoed, *Miles to go before I sleep.*

⟿

SOME MINUTES LATER, teenagers filed from her classroom, suddenly normal and bored again and unmoved by the moving discourse. Thus was teaching, Jude knew. Before Vivi could leave, though, Jude called her back. "Viviana, will you stay a minute?"

Vivi hooked a thumb toward the door. "I have history next hour."

"I'll write you a pass," Jude replied, automatically reaching for her hall pass pad. She didn't wait for the girl to make a second excuse. "Your analysis was...impressive."

"Thanks," Vivi answered, her face brightening at the compliment.

Jude started filling out the hall pass. "Impressive and haunting. I just want to make sure—ever since you and Elijah made that discovery—that you're okay. I imagine that was quite a shock." As little interest as Jude had in the whole drama, she did care about her students, and especially the two of her students who were also her neighbors. It hadn't seemed like Annette or Quinn had made much of a to-do about how things had shaped up, and Jude couldn't be sure if that was a good thing...or a bad thing.

Vivi's eyes turned fiery. "I'm fine. It didn't, like, *bother* me. It was super interesting, actually. I mean, *yeah*. Weird. A little scary, I guess. But it's not *my* back yard. And the skeleton was old anyway."

Jude nodded. "Your thoughts about the poem felt personal. I wondered if you were working with your own experience there."

"Like a *text-to-self* analysis?" Vivi used Jude's instructional language, and they shared a smile over it.

"Yes. Like that."

"I mean—*ashes to ashes* and *dust to dust*, right?" Vivi asked.

"What do you mean?"

"Well, that's sort of how I think about dead bodies. And with Frost hanging out in someone else's forest..."

"Does the forest really belong to any one person?" Jude posited thoughtfully, wishing she'd asked that question for the whole group to hear.

Vivi considered this, clearly giving in to the fact that she'd be more than a minute late to Belinger's class. Jude's next hour was shuffling in behind her, and the white noise of their bags and books and chatter gave Vivi boldness, it seemed. "Yes. It does. That's how the world works. But I guess that contradicts Genesis."

"What do you mean?"

"*Ashes to ashes, dust to dust* originated in Genesis, when God throws Adam and Eve out of the Garden of Eden."

Jude already knew this, but she was surprised to know that Vivi did, too. "You read the Bible?"

"Not exactly. More like Catholic school."

"Me, too," Jude shared, feeling degrees closer to the girl. "So, propriety doesn't jive with the idea that we started as worm food and wind up that way, too?"

"Maybe it doesn't *contradict* it," Vivi replied, appearing to think hard. "But...I guess what I mean to say is that worms don't care about whose woods these are. Whose horse it is. Who's stopping by, so to speak."

Vivi shrugged, plucked Jude's completed hall pass from her fingers, and went to her next class.

Jude, left with her own thoughts and no precocious

teenager to ponder them, connected Vivi's point with her own buried fear. "Worms don't care," she murmured to herself, her back facing the class as she wrote a fresh agenda on the board, "and neither do skeletons."

CHAPTER 7—ANNETTE

After Bill Grange left her house, Annette felt antsy. She could use a stiff drink and a gab session, and with everything going on in her life, it'd be best to round up the troops sooner rather than later.

The next morning, Tuesday, she called a meeting of the minds for that coming Friday night. This would give her the week to handle her new clients, appointments, more unpacking, and so forth.

But just as Annette opened her phone to send out a group text to the neighborhood watch, a news byte sprang across her screen.

Beverly had a new column out. Three more locals, each with a new, juicy question and each with Beverly's dig-deep response.

Annette tapped the notification and found herself

redirected immediately to the first question, which was more of a follow-up than a plea for advice.

DEAR BLUE,

I'm writing to thank you for being so quick to resolve the matter of the Forgotten Christmas Gala. I understand that one such affair is now in the works. For those of us who might find ourselves outside the loop, will you please publish details? What will the gala include? When? Where??? Thank you for taking on an important issue—community involvement!

Truly,

Winters-in-Arizona

ANNETTE SMILED. Winters-in-Arizona was a woman after her own heart. Annette didn't actually know her well, but she knew that they shared an interest in social events, and that was enough for Annette. She flicked her gaze to Beverly's reply.

DEAR WINTERS,

We're working on details now. Early planning includes the holiday lights walk down Main Street (Winter Wonderland on Main), an ice-skating event on Fisherman's Pond north of town, and potentially a community supper. While the first two events are nearly set in stone, the third is up in the air. As you know, Harbor Hills lacks a good-sized venue, which leaves us scrambling for a locale to host a townful of hungry holidayers. If you have any suggestions—or if any reader has a suggestion—please do write in!

FEELING a little stricken by Beverly's tone—so light and cheery and hopeful—Annette gave a moment's thought to what they could do for the final event. Sidewalk sales worked well for this sort of thing in the summertime. Folks meandering up and down Main Street, hitting every shop as they cruised the sales racks. And there were any number of churches that could house a big group at once. Then, of course—what about the high school? She made a mental note to email Darry Ruthenberg, only to realize that Beverly had the easiest access to him—if their togetherness at the harvest party was any indication.

Bubbling with ideas for Shamaine's question, Annette left the news app and returned to her messages, where she tapped out a quick note to her neighbors. *Get-together Friday night? Lots to discuss! Who can host?*

Quinn wrote back first, replying to the whole group. *Ahh. Vivi would kill me. She and Elijah are watching movies here on Friday? I guess? With some friends. Homecoming set a high bar, ha!*

Then came Beverly. *I can't host. Sorry. I'll try to make it, though.*

There was the Beverly Annette knew and loved. Flat tone. Threat of disappointing everyone.

Smirking, Annette spent the rest of the morning awaiting replies from Jude and Elora. Elora would be a questionable addition. They had yet to really include her in their group, but Annette knew it was time. Elora and her trio of towheads were sticking around, and Elora needed female friendships.

After a slow morning of deciding to keep the good china packed and stowed in the basement, Annette eventually heard back from the two missing links.

Jude replied first. *I can make it. Let me know when/where. Thanks.*

At last, a reply came from Elora, but she wrote to Annette in a private text message. *Sounds fun! Wish I could host... Lots going on right now, though...*

Momentarily stunned by the suspense of Elora's message, Annette frowned. She could write back and ask the young woman to explain. She could call her. Or, if it was attention Elora needed, which seemed obvious, Annette could march right over there—to her old house.

And that's just what she did.

But by the time she arrived, just moments later, someone had beat her to the punch.

CHAPTER 8—QUINN

Vivi was on the brink of giving up all hope of extra credit for Belinger's class, and this suited Quinn just fine. She'd much prefer to roll into Christmas with only *Christmas* on her plate. Not added school drama. Quinn was in no place to manage one more thing.

Together, Vivi and Quinn had already accomplished nearly every step of Christmas preparations, and it was only the first week of December. This felt like a triumph. But one point of contention popped up.

Forrest.

Vivi's interest in her mother dating was next to nil, and now that they were talking about some version of a *group* Christmas celebration, Vivi had turned several degrees more vocal.

Their first real fight about it reared its ugly head Tuesday morning over coffee and cereal.

Quinn minded her own business, sipping coffee and skimming yesterday's newspaper and Beverly's adorable column. Currently devouring the second featured question of the column, Quinn silently judged the poor woman who'd written in.

DEAR BLUE FRONT DOOR,

My husband has a history of regifting presents—even to me! He has even made the mistake of giving me a gift certificate to a fast-food restaurant—one that I had originally given him! Help me teach my husband about the spirit of Christmas...spoiling your loved ones and BEING THOUGHTFUL!

—Annoyed Wife

QUINN CRINGED. She wondered why Beverly gave this woman a platform at all, until she read her friend's response.

DEAR ANNOYED WIFE,

It can sting when reality falls short of your expectations. I'm not a licensed marriage
counselor, but that's okay, because your problem is just

as much a human one as a marriage one. Not only does it sound like a failure of communication, but you're also failing to show grace and gratitude. Maybe you two have lost your footing. If you want to feel loved, start by showing him love.

"Mom." Quinn looked up from the newspaper. Vivi stood, hands on her hips, glowering at her mom. "Can we talk?"

"Always," Quinn replied, taking in her daughter's rumpled morning aesthetic. Vivi's hair stood on end, flyaways sprouting like an angel's halo along her hairline. Yesterday's mascara smudged into rings around her eyes. "Did you shower last night?"

Vivi gave her a look. "I'll shower this morning."

"Your sheets, though—" Quinn's compulsion to point out the obvious—or, what *she* felt was obvious—raged in her brain. She'd have to change Vivi's sheets. Going to bed without a shower meant soiled sheets. Not just from makeup, either. From the day's grime. From the germs Vivi had collected at school and wherever else she'd been. And no, Vivi wasn't a dirty person. She was very hygienic. But Quinn's OCD didn't care if Vivi washed her hands when she was supposed to. Quinn's OCD cared that Vivi used a public restroom and sat in the same desk six other kids had sat in over the course of the day. It cared that Vivi wore the same sweatshirt for a week on end without running it through the wash.

"That's not what I want to talk about." Vivi dropped into the chair adjacent to her mom and propped her forearms in front of her. "I want to talk about Christmas."

"What about it?" Quinn tried hard to ignore the invisible germs she could see—the ones transferring from Vivi to the kitchen chair and the tabletop. The ones waiting in her bed. Quinn would be late for work. She'd have to wipe down everywhere Vivi had been. Doorknobs. The staircase rail. Everything.

"Dad wants me to come home and spend Christmas break in Birch Harbor."

Quinn snapped to. "What? No." She frowned and shook her head. "No. We already decided. You'll spend your break here, and I'll take you to Birch Harbor on Christmas Day." This was a perfect arrangement. Matt would get to see Vivi on Christmas Day—the most important day. The traveling would distract Quinn from her woes about having to share her daughter with him. And while Quinn respected Matt to the ends of the earth and valued how strong a father he was...they were divorced. In her mind, Vivi didn't belong to him. Not like she belonged to Quinn.

"But they are having a Christmas thing at the marina. On December 23. I can't miss it. Mercy is begging me to be there."

Mercy was Vivi's best friend from Birch Harbor, and their tie was unbreakable. Missing the Christmas thing at the marina wouldn't change that.

Quinn knew she shouldn't say what she was about to say. She should be more conservative about the blooming relationship between Vivi and Eli. But it was the only rationale she could think to use right now. "What about Eli?"

"He thinks his parents would let him come with me."

"What?" Quinn's plan backfired in a big way. "No. You aren't taking Eli to Birch Harbor. For *Christmas*. Annette would never go for that. Neither would Matt."

"Dad says Eli can stay in the attic rooms at Kate's," Vivi replied, referring to the upstairs guest rooms in her stepmother's home.

Things felt more out of control than ever. She flashed her gaze back to her phone. "I've got an idea," she said, recalling what she'd just seen on her news app. "There's going to be this huge Christmas thing *here*. In Harbor Hills."

CHAPTER 9—ANNETTE

Roman's Jeep sat in their old driveway.

Annette took a minute to process this. *Roman's* Jeep sat in their old driveway. In *Elora's* driveway. How had Annette not noticed this previously? How had she missed the fact that Roman had left—claiming a meeting with clients—only to round the corner of Dogwood and Crabtree Court, turn left on Apple Hill Lane, and left again into 698. Their old house. Elora's house.

She glanced left and right. No one was around. Quinn was at work. Jude was at work. Even Beverly, probably, was at work. Annette, too, should be at work, but inside of her own house. Working on marketing stuff. She'd told Roman that's what she'd be doing.

And here he was, visiting the newly single, young mother on the block. The pretty one who was young enough to bounce back—even from *twins*. Annette found herself wondering what Elora's stomach looked like. A morbid fascination seized her. Was the young mother's skin as wrinkled and puckered as Annette's had been after Elijah came two weeks early by emergency C-section? Was it swollen still? Like a saggy kangaroo pouch—distended but deflated. Or was it taut? Already? Snapping back like a fresh rubber band and attracting the neighborhood husbands like bees to an apple blossom.

Annette shook her hair from her shoulders and ran her fingers along the corners of her mouth, gearing up for a fight. She tugged open the screen door, but before her balled-up fist could make contact with the wood, it swung open, sending her rocking back on her heels and feeling confused to see Elora's wide grin alongside that of Roman's.

A single word slipped through Annette's lips. "What?"

"Annie." Roman grabbed her hand and pulled her in. If this wasn't the best cover-up, Annette didn't know what was. Did he really think he was going to get away with this?

"Roman," Annette replied, glaring hard at him. "I thought you were meeting a client." She turned to Elora, hands on hips and nostrils flared before a phony smile prickled along Annette's thin mouth. "You're not a client now. Are you?"

"Actually, she is," Roman cut in, giving Annette a firm look.

Annette shrank back, closing her eyes and brushing a strand of hair from her forehead. "Sorry, *what*?"

"Annette," Elora said quietly. Sadly. "I'm listing the house."

CHAPTER 10—BEVERLY

Her mother's visit had left Beverly feeling edgy. Bertie had cautioned Beverly against promising the town something elaborate for Christmas, especially a so-called Christmas dinner. "It can't work," Bertie had warned.

Beverly didn't care. With any luck, by the time Christmas rolled around, she'd be living in another place. Returning just for the holidays, begrudgingly, because she owed her mother that much—and now, Darry, too.

But Friday night, everything changed.

Shamaine was back in town—and Shamaine was *never* in Michigan in December. Or January. Or any month after October and before May. Come to think of it, Shamaine hadn't been around since the summer before last, preferring her Tucson patio home for the last eighteen months over the drama of her Harbor Hills street.

Annette had coordinated everything, calling the group together to Shamaine's museum of a house at five in the evening.

Beverly showed up with a half-empty bottle of wine, the best she could do on a week that had been every bit a roller coaster. Good days. Bad. Weird ones. And most troubling, a full evening spent at Darry's house in town. Dinner with drinks after. She'd stayed too late. But by the time she'd gotten home, it had felt too early, somehow. The whole thing was odd and weird and...exciting.

"Bev," Shamaine gasped. "Oh, *Bev*. I haven't seen you since—"

Beverly knew what Shamaine was about to say, so she took the liberty of filling in the sentence for her. "Since before Kayla died." Shamaine hadn't been in town for the funeral but had sent a generous spray of fresh flowers, a chocolate bouquet, and a card so gratuitously touching that Beverly had wanted to burn it. Instead, she had crammed it into the vault of other cards. A sickening stash of mementos that should have been something else. Like all the cards Kayla would have gotten for her high school graduation. Or her wedding. Or her first baby. Instead, the decorative tin box celebrated her death. Not something of her life. No matter what anyone said, when your daughter dies, celebrating her life feels more like a slap in the face than a well-meaning gesture.

"And Tom," Shamaine answered mechanically. Shamaine hadn't been around when they learned the truth about Tom. She didn't know.

Beverly spared her the embarrassment of being out of the loop. "Right."

Shamaine ushered Beverly in with a tight hug, squeezing Bev against her skinny, muscular frame. The benefit of speed-walking year-round was a somehow skeletal, brawny build. Strong but svelte. Shamaine's long, thin fingers wrapped around each of Beverly's arms as they came out of the hug. "I'm so glad you're taking this on."

"Taking what on?" Beverly asked as she moved into the living room, where Shamaine had gathered the others around a table of store-bought goodies. Nothing had left its original plastic container, a testament to the fact that it was Shamaine who'd done much of the purchasing. Shamaine, who'd just arrived in town that Wednesday.

"The Christmas supper." Shamaine beamed the words as she all but pushed Beverly into an open seat next to Elora.

Briefly glancing at the new, young neighbor, Beverly offered a tight smile. "Hi."

Elora reacted in kind, and it occurred to Beverly that the two of them shared much more than a street name. Elora, too, had just lost her husband. In a different way, maybe. Not better or worse. Just different. Different *and* the same.

But Elora hadn't lost her children. No. In fact, in the time since Beverly lost her only child, Elora had created and grown and birthed *two*. Two! Amazing how much could happen in the space of a miserable thirteen months.

"It's wonderful, Bev," Annette agreed. "We're all here to help, in fact."

"Oh." Beverly licked her lips. "You know, it's actually, um, Karen Klepp who is doing the ice-skating rink. And the mayor and town council together with the high school's student council are running the lights thing—the Winter Wonderland."

"And you're doing the supper?" Quinn asked innocently.

"Well, *no*." Beverly tried for a measured tone, but she couldn't help it. The words came out sharp, like a cold smack. Not her town. Not her problem. That's what she was thinking, at least.

"You're not?" Jude looked surprised. "But the newspaper column—"

"I just said I'd facilitate the conversation," Beverly argued. "Not host. I mean, I can't. Not in my house, at least."

"Well, why not?" Annette pried. "It's huge. Plus, the harvest party went so well."

Beverly glanced around at the small group. Save for Shamaine and Elora, they'd comprised her support circle. Her friends. Her *people*. But that didn't matter nearly as much as how it felt to wake up in and go to sleep in the very place where Kayla had spent her whole entire life. "I'm selling my house. I'm moving."

CHAPTER 11—JUDE

"Moving?" Jude asked Beverly. "To where?" She couldn't imagine the stress of packing up a houseful of deceased loved ones' belongings and schlepping them somewhere else. Or worse, selling them off.

Beverly paused a moment before responding. "I don't know yet. Just, *somewhere*. Somewhere else."

"Downsizing?" Annette asked, her eyes glancing off each of the women in turn, as if rounding up the troops for battle.

"Yes," Beverly answered. "Downsizing, for starters. And, well, I just need a change of scenery."

"Do you have a place in mind?" Quinn asked gently.

Beverly shook her head. "Nope. Just somewhere new."

"In town? Out of town?"

Shrugging, Beverly replied, "I don't know."

Jude thought for a moment. "You know," she said, "Elora is moving, too."

Beverly turned to Elora with surprise. "You are?"

Elora gave a short, meek nod, appearing to be uncomfortable with the attention. "I can't manage my house anymore. The bills plus, well, the size of it. I'm not much of an entertainer. When Tad and I bought the place, we had these grand plans of hosting. But now..."

A pang hit Jude's heart. Jude shouldn't have outed the young mother like that. It wasn't her news to share. Then again, if there was an occasion to share such a thing, this was surely it.

Annette jumped in immediately. "That house *is* a lot. I always felt like I was continually preparing for some event." Her eyes flickered. "Gosh, we had so many parties there. Birthdays and Easters. Christmases galore. This will be the first year we don't have our families in town to celebrate." Annette's cheeks pinkened. "Sorry. I don't know why I'm making this about me."

"Let's talk about the Christmas supper," Shamaine redirected. "We need a game plan, and I think I have an idea."

The conversation slowly evolved into a big, cheerful discussion about Christmas cocktails and hors d'oeuvres and what to wear and what music to play, but everyone seemed to be forgetting that they *still* did not have a venue. In Jude's estimation, there was no way this Christmas gala could work. Not the supper aspect, at least. Not in Harbor Hills. Not without the cooperation of some local bigwigs with lots of space and a desire to be charitable. She hated to burst their bubble, but...

"Has anyone contacted the school to host? Maybe Darry would open the gym?"

"Actually, I talked to him," Beverly revealed, looking sheepish. "That was my first idea when I thought I might still take it on." Her tone remained flat. "It's a no-go. They're closing both gyms and the cafeteria over this break for renovations."

"Jude? What about your church?" Annette asked.

"It's too small. You'd think the hall would house as many people as are interested in attending a supper, but the deacon is worried about capacity and this, that, and the other." Jude considered their predicament for a moment. "Maybe we need to think outside of the box."

"You mean, like, take the event to a different town, maybe?" Quinn suggested.

Jude shook her head. "The point is that it's Harbor Hills. It has to be *in* Harbor Hills, right?"

"Home is where the heart is," Annette chimed in.

"Home can be anywhere. Harbor Hills, therefore, can be *anywhere*."

Jude realized at once that Annette was projecting. For Annette—stuck in a house she hated, torn away from the place she wanted so desperately to be her home—she had to believe in this silly adage. That home was a place *inside of you*. Not a place where you lived.

But Jude knew better than that. She knew that a real home *was* a place. Maybe it wasn't the place you thought it should be. Maybe it was too small or too big. Too quiet or too loud. Maybe it wasn't perfect. But in order to have a home, you had to have a *somewhere*. Even if the *somewhere* was all wrong.

In that case, you simply had to make it right.

"I disagree." Jude folded her arms and smirked. "Why pretend?"

Beverly perked up. "Pretend?" Her gaze flitted over the others, a new excitement in her eyes. Like whatever Jude had to say was worthy of something greater than a party-planning session. Like it was big news. Her next breakthrough piece. *Pretending* could be interesting.

Jude refused to indulge her. She refused to explain that home was often nowhere. That some people never really had a home. People like her. "We'll have the gala dinner here, in town." She set her jaw and released her arms, reaching for her drink, like the matter was solved.

But Quinn, ever the anxious one, chimed in. "We don't have a place in town, though, Jude," she replied quietly.

Shamaine added, "It's a problem, Jude."

Jude looked from Shamaine to Quinn to Annette to Beverly to Elora. A sigh filled up her chest, and she released it perfunctorily before lifting her hands and slapping them down on her thighs. "Then, what? We cancel is what we do. You gave it a try, Beverly. But if you can't have it in town, then you have to cancel."

A dramatic sigh escaped someone's mouth, and the group launched into a babbling squabble about Jude's wild suggestion. No one agreed with Jude, but none of them could come to an agreement about anything else, either. They'd arrived at a classic impasse.

And Jude was quickly checking out.

She had little interest in celebrating the holidays—at least with parties—to begin with. Why should she even offer her opinion? Really, it wasn't her problem. It was her friends' problem.

Jude rose and smoothed her sweater down her stomach. Thoughts of the upcoming date night with Dean flickered in her brain then went out like a spent candle. "I've got to get home." It was true. She was missing out on her routine. Liebchen would be furious. "I'm sorry it didn't work out."

CHAPTER 12—THE WOMAN

The days after Christmas were some of her favorite days of the year. The pressure to create a perfect holiday went on hold for what felt like the rest of the woman's life. And really, twelve months—or close to it—could very well *be* the rest of her life. She could die walking down the hall— one misstep, a bad slip, a crack to the head. Or have a massive heart attack in the middle of the night. So far as the woman knew, her parents were in poor health at their deaths. Maybe they both had heart disease, and if they hadn't, they'd have survived the crash. The woman could die right now, on that private boat ride inland.

The Birch Bell rarely, if ever, made winter voyages. It had taken the woman a session with St. Mary's phonebook to locate a private owner who was willing to cross the lake for the sort of fee the woman could offer.

But that mailer—that nondescript advertisement from the Michigan Education Association calling *All Local Educators! The professional development you won't want to miss!*—felt like it meant something. Like it meant something more than just another call to arms for the men and women of the nation who educated America's youth. The timing was perfect: right after Christmas, during the winter break, and before school resumed. The locale was impressive, too: the Henry Ford Museum. Well, technically, according to the online overview, the conference would be held in the Lovett Hall, which was just as well. More intimate. Less pricey, maybe. Who could tell?

But the woman didn't care about any of that. She cared about something to look forward to.

That's why she registered. And after she registered, she planned, even going so far as to mail order—on rush—a new outfit from QVC. She never mail-ordered clothes, and certainly not from QVC, but this felt like an important moment in her life. A *turning* point. A *come to Jesus*, so to speak. Well, *Jesus*, here she was. Ready for her rebirth.

Yes, that was right. The woman would be putting the past behind her. She'd board a stranger's private vessel, head inland, catch a cab, ride to Detroit, and check in at the Dearborn Inn in anticipation of the first education conference she'd ever attend. She'd learn about her vocation—teaching. She'd get away for a while. Maybe even meet new people. Sure, she'd effectively empty her bank account in the process, but that would be the price she'd pay. Quite literally.

There was just one thing to attend to before embarking on her first-ever vacation.

Confession.

CHAPTER 13—QUINN

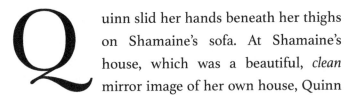uinn slid her hands beneath her thighs on Shamaine's sofa. At Shamaine's house, which was a beautiful, *clean* mirror image of her own house, Quinn felt at peace.

Come to think of it, she felt at peace at every house on Apple Hill Lane...except, sometimes, her own.

Unusually, in her neighbors' homes, Quinn didn't feel the pull to wash her hands after touching things. She didn't have to check the backs of the toilets for dried puddles of urine. Her eyes weren't drawn to brown smudges on the white paint around the doorknobs.

As far as she figured, there wasn't a speck of grime or spot of dirt anywhere in her neighbors' homes.

Or maybe all those things *were* there but Quinn

could look past them. In fact, she didn't feel the need to look for them at all.

It was a strange feeling, this newfound comfort. Was it even comfort at all? Or was it a deeper emotion?

Like, trust?

A thought occurred to her after Jude made her melodramatic exit. "I think Jude's right. If we want to make this happen on such short notice with no other locale, we have to think of other ideas. In fact, maybe we should have it outside."

Beverly bristled. "No one wants to be outside in the cold. It's not a possibility."

"It's almost as though we need more than one location," Annette said, her gaze laser-pointed onto a spot in the ether. Her wheels were turning. The event wheels. She gave her head a shake, but her eyes remained on that pin. "If I were in 698 still, I'd host it. Like an open house." She looked at them. "An open house. That's *it*. You don't need as big a facility if you have an open house. People will drift in and out. It'll take some work, but—"

"Harbor Hills has a population of over five thousand. If even half come, that's two thousand people stomping mud and germs in through your front door. A front door you no longer have." Quinn hated to sound like a wet blanket, but she also knew how sad Annette was to have given up her home. How impotent she felt that she couldn't take the reins on the Christmas dinner.

Quinn noticed that Elora sank back deep in the sofa. Like she wanted to disappear. Quinn didn't want the poor woman to disappear, but it was just that— Elora was in the unfortunate position of being an unwitting villain in the story of Annette's downfall.

Shamaine gave a loud snap of her fingers, and all heads whirled to her.

As boldly and confidently as if she'd been there, on Apple Hill, ever since this little group of friends had formed, she said, "I have a crazy idea."

CHAPTER 14—ANNETTE

Shamaine's idea *was* crazy, and that's why Annette loved her. It was a huge risk—and it required a lot of moving parts. As well as Roman's cooperation. Roman's cooperation was the key factor. He had the knowhow to pull it off, but first, three of the neighbors would have to come to an agreement about their futures.

And getting six women on the same page could prove impossible.

But that was the least of their worries. There was one other obstacle that could derail the entire thing.

Annette returned home after the little neighborhood council meeting, shuffled through the file of business cards she kept in her junk drawer, and found what she was looking for. *Detective William Grange.*

He answered on the first ring.

"Grange."

"Bill, it's Annette Best."

"Annette," he answered in surprise. "Everything okay?"

"Yes, yes," she rushed to answer. "I'm calling about the case. The body, you know."

Of course, he knew, she realized, and she didn't wait for his response. "Bill, there's a...business situation that might affect your work."

"A business situation that might affect my work? As in—our investigation?" She could hear his jeering smile—almost laughter—but she was quick to brush it off.

"Yes. Elora Beckett is putting her house up for sale."

"She can't do that just yet, I'm afraid," Bill replied. "Once we ID the body and come close to a cause and manner of death, the investigation will only heat up."

"You've collected half the soil in the yard," Annette pointed out, exasperated.

"Doesn't matter. We might need a warrant to search the house. Truth be told, Annette, you never should have moved out to begin with. It was a major disruption in the process."

Annette huffed. "Whether I'm living there or the Becketts are, you aren't going to find evidence among anything in the house. If it's *evidence* you're looking for, Bill, look somewhere else."

"And why's that, Annette?" He was growing more irritated by the moment.

Annette revealed her trump card. "Because the families of Apple Hill Lane have retained a lawyer."

CHAPTER 15—SHAMAINE

Shamaine gathered the gals together at the Dorgendorf. It was the only suitable restaurant in town, after all. Especially for a party of six.

"Here's the plan," she began, all eyes on her. Dang, it was good to be back. As much as Shamaine hated ice and treacherous roads, she had also grown sick of the Phoenix heat. A winter visit was exactly what she needed. There was another reason she was back, but well, that was a private one.

Anyway, this trip home had been so good that Shamaine started to wonder if she might just stick around longer term. Heck, it might even drag her out of retirement. Who knew? She wrapped her strong, manicured fingers around her drink, a cream-colored porcelain mug simmering with mulled wine.

She cut to the chase about what she thought her neighbor gals ought to do.

"It's like musical chairs but with houses. Then, once each of you is in the *right* house—which we will make happen lickety-*split*, ladies. And I mean"—she snapped the fingers of her left hand, her oversize engagement rock sparkling in the moody, low light of the dining room—"*fast*. We'll all pitch in. With the moving, I mean." Shamaine took a drink, but the others, normally chatty, remained quietly entranced with her.

"Then," she went on, "once everyone is settled, we can move forward with plans for the Christmas dinner."

Appetizers arrived—fried calamari, the good kind. Shamaine eyed it, then she eyed the other women. "Well? Are we eating or aren't we?" She wiggled her weight forward on the suede bench and spotted the best hunk of battered mini squid in the bunch. She stabbed it with her fork and cupped the other hand beneath, transferring the delectable morsel to her left and sliding it with her middle finger smack-dab in the center of Elora's plate. "Have you had this before?" Something told Shamaine she'd predicted correctly, and that prediction was confirmed when Elora squinted at the hunk of fried meat.

Elora bit her lower lip. She shook her head.

Shamaine cackled. "Don't get your shorts in a twist,

El. It's not like escargot or, heck, even mussels. Although I'd argue mussels are far milder than calamari. I mean, you don't even taste a mussel. It's just the wetness that gets to some people."

Annette added, "I'd say caviar is the fanciest weird food I ever ate. At our rehearsal dinner. Roman's folks footed that bill."

"Caviar straight up or on blini?" Shamaine and Annette shared a taste for the finer things in life. In fact, Shamaine shared at least one trait or experience with nearly every one of the women on Apple Hill. The present women, that was. Back in the day, when Brenda Caputo lived next door, the same couldn't be said.

Annette really did appreciate the good life, just like Shamaine. Annette liked a neat, beautiful home. She liked perfection. She liked image. There was nothing wrong with that. Shamaine called it high personal standards.

With Elora, Shamaine shared height—or lack thereof. A silly thing to share, but...short women were a special breed. They were more than their size, and they knew it. It bonded them. An unspoken bond. At five foot two, Shamaine was on the taller side of short, but her girth made her seem even shorter. Elora had to be no higher than five-one. They'd giggled together over one another's squatness just as soon as they'd met earlier that week. Short women stuck together.

Of course, *all* women—good women, at least—stuck together.

As for Quinn, it was easy to see the commonality with Shamaine: their shared sense of great style. Quinn could have walked off the pages of a Land's End catalogue. Maybe even Ann Taylor, especially that night. She seamlessly pulled off chic black skinny jeans, dark leather booties, and an olive-colored blouse. Individually, the pieces were *whatever*. Together, though, she looked almost as good as Shamaine in her wide-leg trousers with a structured berry-red sweater. The only real difference, stylistically, between Shamaine and Quinn was their stature. Quinn was a stalk of celery, elegantly thin, and Shamaine was more like a plum, deliciously round. Shamaine didn't mind. They complemented one another.

With Beverly, the unity was a depressing one, but impenetrable. Shamaine's son, Tyler, had died at the tender age of twenty-five. His five-year deathiversary was coming up on December 31. Shamaine hadn't mentioned it, but that was the big, fat, secret reason she'd returned to Harbor Hills. *Not* the Phoenix heat.

And *not*—surprisingly, perhaps—because of the Christmas Gala. But Shamaine knew that in life, people didn't always have to have all of your truth. You got to curate what they knew about you. It was one of those things that she hadn't learned until after the nightmarish tragedy that was Tyler's passing. That her life was hers and hers alone, and if she was going to share bits and pieces of it with others, then she'd pick what she shared. It wasn't going to do them or her any good to get the full picture. Especially in a case like this, when the truth was a critically private matter. A scandal. In some circles, a *crime*, even.

There was just one of the Apple Hill women with whom Shamaine had nothing in common. Or, at least, nothing she knew of.

Jude.

A truly closed book, Jude must also have believed in curating her own image, because all that Shamaine could see of it was a choosy divorcee with an oversized black cat and a penchant for religion.

A realization seized Shamaine. *That's* what she had in common with Jude.

Self-preservation.

Self-preservation could explain quite a bit in life. Like, for example, why Jude had left their get-together the other night. Shamaine decided then and there to remove all fault from the woman. Something was hurting her. Something was keeping her severe like she was. And Shamaine wasn't about to shame someone like that. She had had enough of her own shame to deal with. She was sick of the very notion of *shame*.

The   conversation   had   returned   to   plans

surrounding the Christmas dinner. Shamaine tuned in on Jude, who looked edgy.

"I thought we agreed," Jude said with suspicion, "the dinner is out. It's a nonstarter."

Shamaine shook her head. "None of us agreed that. You just said it. Then you left." No sense in painting the truth in soft shades of a different color. Might as well have it all out. On the table. A good bicker could really spur on a good friendship anyway.

"I'm a little lost," Beverly piped up. "What do our living arrangements have to do with the Christmas dinner?"

Shamaine grinned, her lipstick-covered lips stretching like the Cheshire cat's. "I'll tell you."

CHAPTER 16—BEVERLY

Beverly liked Shamaine. She had no reason to like Shamaine, who was brash and bossy. But there was an honesty in her. A grit. A will to survive.

Plus, Beverly knew about Tyler. And even though Shamaine didn't *know* Beverly knew, she was in the loop on exactly what had happened to him. No one else in town knew. Beverly did.

She leaned in closer as Shamaine recounted her idea of the perfect small-town Christmas.

"Picture it," Shamaine commanded, her hands framing an invisible tableau. "Christmas on Apple Hill Lane, a new holiday tradition." Her voice was embarrassingly booming through the dim restaurant.

Most of their table oohed in warm appreciation.

But Beverly remained skeptical, and from the looks of her expression, so did Jude.

But Beverly was the one with good reason to feel anxious about celebrating Christmas. Not only had she barely gotten through the one-year anniversary of Kayla's and Tom's deaths, but Kayla's birthday was in February, looming as heavily as if it were a week away.

Beverly quietly wondered if there would ever be a time when she wasn't dreading something, when she would look forward to something again?

She snuck her phone out of her purse and tapped out a quick text to Darry—the only person who felt like a safe venting space in a swimming pool of holiday-hungry humans.

We're only doing the lights festival, right? Not sure I can stomach ice-skating.

He replied immediately. *Isn't there a community dinner event?*

Her eyes flicked around herself. Shamaine, Annette, Quinn, and even meek Elora were immersed in a wobbly, block-party-style idea. Beverly didn't understand. It was *winter,* for Pete's sake.

She texted Darry back. *Looking doubtful.*

If a walk down Main Street is all I'm gonna get with you, I'll take it.

Beverly didn't want to smile. She tried hard to stop the smile from forming on her mouth as she stared at the screen on her thigh. *I'll keep you posted if the dinner comes together, but don't hold your breath.*

"Beverly? What do you say?" Annette asked. "Are you interested?"

Beverly shoved the phone down deep in her purse and looked up. "Sorry, I just don't see how this thing can work. I don't understand—you want us to have a Christmas dinner on Apple Hill Lane?"

The tinkling of their forks and spoons against their plates paused, and silence crested over the table.

She blinked. "Interested in what?"

"In selling your house and buying mine."

CHAPTER 17—JUDE

It was laughably ridiculous—all of it. Shamaine's idea that three of her neighbors would play musical houses was the most ridiculous part. Her other idea that they could somehow pull off Christmas dinner on a town street rather than in a proper event venue was almost as bad.

Jude could calculate all of the missteps. Firstly, if Elora couldn't afford her current home, how would she afford Beverly's? Yes, Beverly's was smaller. Yes, the lot was smaller, too. Plus it didn't have as expansive a second floor...but still.

And if Beverly were trying to make a clean break of Harbor Hills, why should she want to move just up the street? Barely a block over? Not *even* a block over? Only if her goal was to simply leave behind her home—not the area. If it were Jude, she would want to get out of Dodge. Right?

Surely she wouldn't want to stick around in the haunting history of her life?

Then again...

But of course, what about Annette? She couldn't afford 698 Apple Hill before—how would she move back into it? Unless her business rebrand was so miraculous that she could swing it. No way. No way had she and Roman turned things around in a matter of a month—less than that. And even if they had, would it be very smart to test the waters of their former extravagance so early on? Wouldn't it be wiser to sit tight and just *see*?

Jude wasn't one for taking risks, and all of this felt like one big risk.

She thought about these women and her own place on their street. She thought about what they meant to her. What she might mean to them. She'd been honest at Shamaine's house, and that had gotten her—and them—nowhere. Should she strive for honesty once more or just leave it be?

What difference did it make to her if her neighbors bumped in and out of one another's houses?

Oh. Right. The Christmas Gala. If Jude didn't speak up, she'd likely be roped into participating in *that*, too. And Jude really wasn't interested in participating in that. In fact, she wasn't interested in participating in

Christmas whatsoever. At *all*. After spending the past many years putting on a happy face with Gene, she looked forward to a reprieve. She didn't have to get a tree. No lights to hang. No seasonal towels to painstakingly drag out, launder, fold, hang. None of those little things that would all need to be *un*done twelve days after the birth of Christ.

Nope.

All Jude cared about now was her Advent table, complete with candles and a simple, wooden Advent calendar. That was *it*, and it was refreshing. Refreshing to be free from all that noise in her house. All that busyness that made her house something it wasn't. Something it would never be again.

CHAPTER 18—QUINN

Quinn found herself relaxed at dinner. Relaxed enough to see that she wasn't the only one among her group of friends privately harboring something —guilt, fear...*secrets*.

They'd finished their appetizers and had now moved on to the main course. She wasn't that hungry, and Forrest was coming later for drinks. All on account of Vivi's decision to visit Birch Harbor for the weekend. A protest, apparently.

She felt compelled to share this thing—this thing that upset her. "Shamaine, you're divorced." She said this as mildly as she could, but even if she'd been indelicate about it, it wouldn't matter—Shamaine loved to talk. "Did you share custody of your children with your ex?"

Shamaine froze, but only momentarily. Quinn was convinced she hadn't even seen it. That she was wrong. Like when the electricity in your house flickered so imperceptibly that maybe it didn't flicker at all.

Maybe a storm wasn't descending.

Maybe the lights would stay on and the television would continue to blare. The furnace would run.

Nothing would change.

But then...they were at an impasse right now. Elora was nervous that her bills wouldn't drop enough in Beverly's house. Beverly was nervous that Dogwood Drive wasn't far enough away. Annette was nervous that Roman wouldn't agree to jump back into the world of bigger bills.

Something had to change. Had to shake them loose.

Quinn took a tentative step onto the thin ice of her inner pain. "I'm having trouble with Vivi again." She sank into herself, her body deflating, releasing the air it'd been saving up for that moment when she wouldn't be able to breathe because of all the hurt.

Shamaine blotted her red lips. "Yes," she said. "My children split their time here and with their dad. Fifty-fifty."

"You didn't have majority custody?" Annette asked, appalled.

The expression on Shamaine's face was unflinching. Obstinate, even. "See, now, that's the problem with parents today. They hog their children, keeping them all to themselves. It's a selfish thing, and divorced parents are all the more selfish when they believe so firmly that one over the other has more right to more time with the child. When both parents *can* provide for the child, then it should be an even-steven arrangement. Just as it would be in a happy, whole home where the mom and dad are still together."

Quinn sorted through Shamaine's rant about the subject, finding her place in it. Splitting custody? She couldn't agree with Shamaine. If Quinn agreed, then she'd be a hypocrite. She was hogging Vivi, after all. For this conversation to continue, to be productive, she'd have to admit as much. So, she did.

"I want my daughter to be with me. I want her to *want* to be with me. I have full custody, and that's how it should be. Right now, Vivi visits her dad sparingly, but *he* had full custody before. Maybe that makes it even?" Quinn knew she sounded like a brat, but how could she possibly say she didn't want Vivi around all the time? What kind of mother *admitted* she needed a break from her kids? Or that her kid needed to see the other parent? Not an obsessive one like Quinn.

A better mother than Quinn, probably. More balanced. Healthier. More mature.

Shamaine shrugged. "Why don't you want to share her with her dad? Doesn't he want her half the time?

Why should anyone get all of her? Why shouldn't she get more of both of you?"

Annette nudged Quinn beneath the tabletop then spoke. "Vivi and Quinn's is a special circumstance."

Elora surprised them all when she asked, "What's so special about divorce and child custody arrangements? Half the country does it."

All eyes shifted to the youngest among them. The smallest.

Quinn recalled Elora's recent drama and felt degrees worse for her than she felt for herself, which was saying something, because Quinn felt pretty miserable for herself.

"What if Tad wanted your boys to stay with him over Christmas? At his parents' house? That's where he is, right? Hiding out after his scandal?" Quinn was rarely one to call someone out so flagrantly but, well, Elora *did* ask.

Elora's face froze over. "That's different."

"How?" Annette asked. Annette was Quinn's best friend, and Quinn knew this was her picking sides. They shouldn't be ganging up, though. Not against Elora. The young, new mother. The one whose husband was in the throes of a criminal investigation into his inappropriate relationships with female students. Annette softened. "Quinn's point is that custody issues are supremely personal, I think. It's one reason those who *do* stay together *stay*. They fear the repercussions for their children."

"And for themselves." Jude said this so quietly she might not have said it at all.

Quinn squinted at her. "You don't have children."

Jude shook her head. "And I never will."

Shamaine chortled. "*Child-free* before it was trendy, eh, Judy?"

"It's Jude, and no. I'd have loved to have children. Just wasn't in the cards." Something more boiled behind Jude's eyes. Quinn could sense this. Something dark.

And the only way they were going to get Jude to open up—or Elora to fit in, or Shamaine to stick around—was to up the ante. Raise the stakes.

Quinn knew exactly what to say.

The truth. Painful and humiliating and crippling.

But if she said it, she'd be free. And so would her friends. Something would loosen up in everyone. Facades would crumble.

True, deep friendship would build in its place.

Quinn blinked away the threat of a tear. "I don't know if Matt is Vivi's father."

CHAPTER 19—THE WOMAN

She would leave for her conference the following day. With everything packed—including her new, rush-order pantsuit and paired kitten heels—the woman made her way from her room at St. Mary's into the church.

Once there, she took the familiar path through the interior doors, to the right, behind the last pew and into the dark, wooden corner, where a second, short corridor would carry her directly to her destination.

"Father Dan," she murmured. The priest, whose head was—assumedly—dipped in prayer, looked up.

He adjusted his eyeglasses, then lowered his head again, gesturing to the confessional.

She stepped into the far booth and knelt in front of the wicker screen, her eyes squeezed shut, breath shallow.

When Father Dan didn't immediately speak, she fumbled through a second greeting. "Um. Good evening, Father."

"Good evening, my child."

As far as he knew, she was here for her regular, weekly confession. She'd list off a rudimentary set of offenses. Snapping at students. Ignoring the headmaster during meetings. Opting out of Adoration due to slothfulness. That sort of thing.

But he was wrong.

She signed the cross and spoke low, her voice trembling so hard that it caught in her throat over every other word. "In the name of the Father, and of the Son, and of the Holy Spirit."

Together, they chanted, "Amen."

Then it was his turn. "May the Lord help you confess your sins."

She took a gulping breath of air, but instead of oxygen, a sob crawled down her throat, going the wrong way and choking her up. Hard.

But confession isn't about sympathy or compassion. It's about release.

And so, she let go.

CHAPTER 20—ANNETTE

Annette's jaw dropped at Quinn's bombshell.

Matt might not be Vivi's father.

What!?

How had Annette not known this? How did *Quinn* not even know for sure? How could it even be *possible* that there was a question? Quinn was so...perfect. Tidy and meticulous and careful. Certainly *not* the sort of woman who had any questions of paternity, for goodness' sake. It sounded so *Ricki Lake*. Or *Jerry Springer*.

Her hand instinctively flew to Quinn's on top of the table. Squeezing, she gave voice to the words on everyone's mind.

"You're joking, Quinn."

Shamaine cackled—*the gall*—and added, "Looks like every single person here has some sort of drama in her goldarn life. Look at us. A fine bunch of freaks."

Annette shot Shamaine a sharp look, and Jude hissed, "*Shamaine, please.*"

Beverly leaned forward, Annette saw, and if she'd had her reporter's notepad, Annette figured she'd have flipped to a fresh sheet and started up a page of shorthand on poor Quinn.

But if Quinn had *cheated*, how could any one of them sympathize with that?

Annette's first instinct may have been to jump to such salacious conclusions, but she swallowed that down and squeezed Quinn's hand once more. "What happened, Quinn?"

Quinn looked like she might throw up but managed to attempt an explanation, nonetheless. "We weren't married. When I got pregnant. It was a shotgun wedding. I mean, we'd been together for a while, Matt and me."

Annette nodded, encouraging her. The others remained silent. Expectant. As respectful as you could hope for from a group of gossips such as themselves.

"Well, while we were together, something happened." Her voice shook hard, and Annette's gut swirled in anticipation of what Quinn might say next. They must have all been thinking the same thing. The air was sucked from their nook in the restaurant. Stillness fell across them.

Quinn squeezed her eyes shut and gripped the

edges of the table. A thrumming vibration commenced. Annette knew that Quinn was bouncing her knees as fast as they would go. "Something *happened*." Her eyes flew open. "But it was my fault."

CHAPTER 21—SHAMAINE

Shamaine knew *exactly* where this was going, and she didn't like it one bit. But if there was a woman at their table prepared to handle such a revelation, she was as good as any.

She gave Quinn a hard once-over, taking in the perfectly put-together blonde woman. Quinn could have been a model. She could have been anything she wanted to be with those icy blues and the perfect tan and the Nordic American look. Unlike Shamaine, who got her way by sheer force, Quinn probably could have relied on looks alone to get any job done. And yet she was articulate. She was unassuming. Quiet. Serious. Kind. And smart. *So* smart.

But if she was so smart, and if Shamaine's assumption about Quinn's suggestion was accurate, then...

Shamaine shifted her weight and pinned her forearms on the table, tenting her hands downward, toward Quinn. A lawyerly pose if ever there was one. "You were assaulted."

CHAPTER 22—BEVERLY

Beverly had expected Quinn to say this—they all had—but when Shamaine dropped that sentence like a hammer, she couldn't help but gasp.

Of all the tragedies in the world, surviving death was one of the most brutal. Beverly had survived the death of her husband. Of her very own *daughter*. Her teenage daughter. She knew the brutality on a personal, deep level.

Quinn, if Shamaine's guess was right, had survived the most dehumanizing offense against womankind. Humankind, actually.

Beverly put away all thoughts of scandal and drama, and her face fell into a sad slope of emotion. "Is it true?"

Quinn's face cleared of the greenish-white hue, and color returned to her cheeks. As if the worst was over. Maybe it was.

She dropped her head, and her answer came swiftly and low. "No."

CHAPTER 23—JUDE

Appalled and bewildered, Jude had little to offer this conversation. What did Quinn mean? Had she been abused? *Raped?* Or hadn't she? Was Shamaine right? And if not, then what? She'd *cheated* on Matt Fiorillo? Both scenarios felt troublesome but at far ends of the spectrum, of course. It was one thing to break a commitment. It was another to fall prey like that. To be taken advantage of. To have your own body violated...

Visions of Gene flashed through her mind. Unwelcome ones. Ones that turned Jude's stomach into waves of queasiness.

They were *getting real*, as her students would say. They were getting too personal and *too* real, and Jude worried that if she stuck around any longer, she'd have to divulge her deepest, darkest secrets, too. All the bad things that had happened to *her*.

All the bad things that, in reality, were *her* fault, too. Just like whatever had happened to Quinn was *her* fault.

Jude had two choices. Run away again, just like she had at Shamaine's house.

Or stay and involve herself.

Another image swept into her brain, further complicating her decision.

Dean. Dean, who was patient and kind and hoping to join her again at Mass the following Sunday. Her queasiness returned. How could Jude manage all of this? All of this pain and weirdness and discomfort?

And...hope?

She couldn't.

Not alone.

"Quinn, we all have pasts," Jude heard herself say. It was an out-of-body experience. Jude nodded to Beverly. "Beverly does." Then Shamaine. "Shamaine." And she continued around the table, indicating Elora and Annette with a careful dip of her chin. "We all do."

Quinn stared at Jude, who felt hot under the attention. She had to force herself to hold the look and return an expression of comfort. Of assurance. After a beat, it was as if it was just the two of them—Quinn and Jude in a cloud of their own inner thoughts—and Quinn's face softened. "It happened *so* long ago. Sometimes, I don't even know if my memories are real. Or if I've...conjured them. Does that make any sense?"

Jude smiled. "It makes perfect sense." And it did. Jude herself often wondered if what she remembered from her own long and winding history was real.

Because if it *was* real, then what did that say about *Jude*?

CHAPTER 24—THE WOMAN

"Forgive me, Father, for I have sinned. It has been some weeks since my last confession."

Father Dan waited in silence for her to go on.

It took every morsel of energy and courage for her to do just that. To swallow her sobs. She thought she might begin with warm-up sins, figuring that if she seemed normal, then the big reveal could easily get lost in the mix. Squeezing her eyes shut hard, she tried to conjure up every minor infraction from the preceding week.

But nothing recent came to mind.

Instead, a memory did.

A warm, holiday memory plucked like a slow-falling snowflake from her very early childhood.

For Christmas, when she was about five, Santa had

delivered a puppy. A real live puppy! Complete with a big red bow and a brand-new water bowl and leash. Everything. One day, the puppy went missing. After a frostbite-inducing search in the yard and down the street, the family had been prepared to draw up fliers and alert the pound. But as that unfolded, the girl escaped to her bed, where a mound of stuffed animals held court. Among them, nestled in the very center, was the new puppy, still as a toy and snoring. Entirely camouflaged among the rest of the girl's hoard. A big, important thing that blended in with lots of little things somehow.

It was a good day. A day where a bad thing wasn't bad after all. It was just one of the many good things in her life then. And the bad thing had been nothing more than a fleeting panic. A mistaken belief, in fact.

The woman's attention now returned to the priest's quiet presence beyond the wicker screen.

This was nothing like that emotional day. This was much different.

"Father," she started, bolder now. Detached, even, from that sensitive, weeping woman racked with guilt. Prepared to make her peace with what she'd done. What she *hadn't* done. "I haven't been to confession since before Thanksgiving." She added this note as a warning.

"Most people don't confess weekly," he answered.

"I do," the woman said. "But there's a reason I haven't been."

His silence indicated he was listening.

She went on. "The reason I haven't been to confess is because I've committed a great sin. Perhaps the greatest of sins, Father."

"No one sin is greater than any other. All sins are equal, and for all of your sins you shall be absolved if you repent."

Confession wasn't meant to be a counseling or therapy session. Normally, the priest wasn't an active communicator during the whole thing. Normally, he just waited her out, then gave her her assigned penance. But she could tell that he could tell how much she was struggling.

"Father"—the woman's voice shook once again —"I've done a terrible thing."

CHAPTER 25—QUINN

"When Matt and I were dating, we were hot and cold, you know? Good days and bad, and then it came to this point where we had to give each other space."

"A break," Jude encouraged Quinn.

She paused. "At first, actually, I wanted to end it. For good."

"But?" Annette asked.

"He was conflicted. We both were, really. But Matt got me to agree to just one week. A week off." She dropped her face into her hands and said more, but she knew it was unintelligible. Even so, her friends gave her a moment before asking her to repeat what she'd said.

It was Jude who pushed her to reiterate her words.

Jude, who was unpeeling her for them all to see. Jude, who was coming to life over Quinn's great, big, scary confession. It was an oddity—*she*, Jude, was an oddity. And now maybe more. Why was she so interested in this? Did it have to do with her history in Birch Harbor? Her history with *Matt*? Did Judith Carmichael, *Jude Banks*, know Matt? Apart from the usual small-town acquaintance?

Or was her interest self-serving? Quinn swallowed hard and tried to refocus herself. She locked eyes with Jude and Jude alone. "We were allowed to do whatever we wanted. And...I *knew* he saw someone else. And so I did, too."

She could feel her chest and neck go splotchy. Her fingers were typing out a string of affirmations against her thighs. *I feel good. I feel great. I feel wonderful. I feel good. I feel great. I feel wonderful. I feel good I feel great I feel wonderful. IfeelgoodIfeelgreatIfeelwonderful.*

Quinn knew her bouncing legs were shaking the whole table. The ice in their water glasses clinked. Silverware shook against plates. But Quinn didn't care about any of that. She just cared about Vivi. What Vivi knew. What Vivi did not know. What Matt knew. What Matt did not know.

And now, for whatever reason, what her *friends* knew.

What they did not know.

That Quinn was not perfect. That Quinn had made a very bad decision.

Maybe even that Quinn was a very bad person.

CHAPTER 26—THE WOMAN

It took the woman some time to recover from the sobs. Minutes on end. As she wept, Father Dan remained silent, and once she felt ready to go on, she couldn't be certain he was still there and willing to hear her. Plus, what if other parishioners were waiting on that back pew? Praying until they were out of prayers and wondering *who* was sobbing in the confessional and more to the point, *why*?

"Father?" she whimpered pathetically.

"Go on," he answered, more alert than he'd been when they began.

"Will this confession stay between us? What if—what if I've broken the law? Will you report me to the police?"

"This confession goes from your lips to God's ears. Your heart to His. Whatever you say here is said to lift your burden, child. Your confession to me is privileged between us, but it is not for me to know your sin. It is for you to repent and offer penance to God. It is not the law that will provide you mercy. It is our Father who will do that. Your sin is safe here."

"It's long. It's a long...story." She grappled with that word.

"God is patient."

"What about others who are waiting for you? Maybe I should go last?"

"You arrived first. It's your time now. If you're ready, God is ready."

His reply was enough. Assured that she'd be safe to unload on Father Dan, the woman began.

"I've shared very little of my life with the girls here at the school. They know I attended St. Mary's. They know I was called to teach after a difficult upbringing. They don't know that I have family remaining. A grandfather in Harbor Hills. He survived my grandmother's passing just recently." She paused, debating briefly whether to explain the woman's untimely death. It was best she did. God had better have it all. From her lips to His ears, right? Then again, wasn't God all-knowing? Didn't he already...*know* all of this? And if so, what point was there in confessing?

Ah yes, to unburden one's soul. The woman needed that more than she needed air. To free herself from the guilt. The burning guilt. To say it aloud so that she could tell herself she'd said it. She'd *confessed*.

"She struggled seriously with depression. She was committed to a psychiatric facility, even. She was suicidal. When she died, I didn't attend her funeral." This alone might have been enough for a hearty Catholic confession. But it was merely the tip of the iceberg. "She was an unhappy woman when I knew her, when she took me in." The woman rushed to add, "Well, she didn't take me in, you see. When my parents died, Nana and Grandad kept me for a short time before sending me here. Anyway, Nana was always cruel, and when she passed, I took it for suicide, and since...well, since I didn't feel close to her, my emotions about it were raw. I didn't go. I didn't ask after her much, and so I just figured she'd taken her own life. That itself is such a horrid thing. I had a lot of hate in my heart about it all. Only later did I go home to visit Grandad, and he suggested there was more to Nana's death."

She swallowed, waiting for a fresh round of tears to come. When it did not, she pushed ahead. "At one point, Grandad said Nana's death was some sort of *accident*. He used that word—*accident*—but it wasn't what he meant. Not really."

Tremors crawled up her spine, seizing her neck in a painful cramp. She was getting closer. She had to get through. Had to work through this. The woman rolled her shoulders back and licked her lips and focused on telling the story to God. Not to Father Dan. Not to anyone else. Just Him. It was her explanation, and she needed Him to know what was in her heart. In her mind.

"Grandad and I were slowly growing close, you see. I didn't want to ruin what we were building. Things were improving, and I had family for the first time in a long time. And a home, too. See, that was the thing— since my parents died, I'd never had a home to go to, and once Grandad and I were getting along so well, I finally had one and—" She was rambling, and a sob caught up to her. She tamped it down with a careful swallow. "He told me there was an accident in one of the properties they owned. A fall. A push and a fall. I *knew* what he was saying. I knew it in my heart, but I refused it. I told him he was wrong. I told Grandad he had it all wrong—that she wasn't well. I asked him; I said, 'Grandad, she got upset and took a bad fall. Right? *Right*, Grandad?'

"He was numb, maybe, I don't know. He just nodded. That was the story he gave to the police, too. And there was no autopsy or medical examination. It was too easy. This angry, elderly woman who'd only just been released from the hospital. She traveled alone to Apple Hill Lane. Without Grandad. They'd had a fight. She went *home*, and when she got there, Grandad told me, she was locked out. They owned the whole street, but she was locked out of her house. But she had spare keys to their other properties. That was when Nana learned the truth—that Grandad had started selling the homes the Carlson family had built. He'd sold them right behind her back, forging her signature or something. He'd rented out every last home except for one, and that was the only one Nana's spare key would open. Because he'd even changed the locks on six-nine-six. On her own house. If you can even believe that. But I did because I knew how awful she was, and I felt bad for Grandad. I figured he was right to do something with the properties. It was the only way. So she went into the house at the center of the street, this gorgeous brick colonial house, and when she got inside, someone followed her in, Grandad said. The person who owned the house next door. They'd seen Nana arrive and figured her for a burglar, and there was an argument and a hard shove. She hit her head on the corner of a pony wall in the foyer of that house.

"Grandad drove to town right away, but it was too late. He buried her that weekend. I didn't go."

The woman eased back, resting her behind on her heels and taking a breath.

Father Dan cleared his throat. "For your penance—"

But she shot back up on her knees. "Wait. I'm...I'm not done. There's more."

CHAPTER 27—ANNETTE

The server, inane as he was, interrupted them with dessert menus.

Annette began to shoo him off. She was desperate to tell Quinn that Quinn was not a bad person. That she was a human being. And that whatever she'd done wrong, she could fix it. She really could.

But before Annette could successfully rid them of the intrusion, Shamaine slapped her hands down on the table. "Dessert is *exactly* what we need," she declared. "And dessert drinks, too. A round of hot toddies and a pumpkin pie for the table. Don't cheap out on the whipped cream, either," she threatened the server, who scurried off.

Annette just laughed and shook her head.

"Shamaine, I'm not sure if people are glad that you're back in town or scared."

"Hopefully a bit of both," Shamaine replied before turning to Quinn. "Whatever you've done, it's nothing that pie can't fix."

Annette let out a breath she didn't realize she'd been holding. Ultimately, Shamaine was probably right. She laughed and added, "Unless you killed someone."

The table tensed briefly before Quinn let out a short laugh and flicked hair from her eyes. "Luckily, it's not *that* bad."

There was a hum of errant conversation while the server returned with drinks and pie, and Annette turned to Jude to get a read on her take of the whole thing.

But when she looked at Jude, the woman was iced over. Her face stiff and sunken, like she'd fallen onto a mortician's table. Her hands knitted together so tightly Annette felt the compulsion to pry them apart.

"Jude," she said, gripping the woman's shoulder and giving a gentle shake. Jude's face twisted into deeper grooves as she slowly turned to Annette. She didn't say anything. Just shook her head. Annette glanced at the others. Everyone had started in on pie—even Quinn, whose tapping and bouncing and typing and oddities had all quieted, miraculously. Annette lowered her voice. "Jude, what is it?"

Jude opened her mouth to reply, but nothing came out. She just shook her head again, then swallowed.

"Do you know something?"

Jude's tongue darted through her impeccably lined and painted lips. In and out. Another swallow. Her face broke and she nodded.

Annette, now aghast and agog and all things hungry and interested, turned furtive. "About Quinn?"

CHAPTER 28—THE WOMAN

Father Dan remained quiet again, allowing her to finish her confession once and for all.

And so, she did.

Shifting her weight across her knees, which had gone numb with pressure, she sucked in a deep breath, then let it all out.

"After Grandad told me what happened and I convinced him it really was an accident, that it wasn't foul play or whatever he was suggesting, things went back to normal between us. He seemed happier, even. Then I arrived this year for Thanksgiving—I always go home for the holidays. But this particular Thanksgiving, you see, Grandad wasn't alone. There was someone else there. I was...caught off guard. He introduced me, and that was when I learned Grandad had secrets. Big ones."

She closed her eyes and again rocked back on her heels, rubbing her kneecaps and wondering how she could possibly go and enjoy a conference after all of this. Wouldn't something more happen? Wouldn't she finish all of this and be carted directly to an interrogation room?

But it was too late now. Momentum carried her forward. She leaned back in.

"I'd heard of this woman who'd gone missing—read about her in the papers. Knew the family, even. Or knew *of* them. Tempers. It was *her*. The missing woman."

Father Dan made a noise that sounded quite like a gurgle. "This is confidential, your confession. But I have to interrupt to say that if you share information with me that could help me prevent a sin, I'm obliged to—"

"It's too late for that," she replied in a shameful whisper. "She's dead."

CHAPTER 29—SHAMAINE

Shamaine sucked the last bit of pumpkin-flavored whipped cream from her fork, then stabbed it in Quinn's direction. They'd all let her off the hook. Good food did that to even the greatest of gossips. It couldn't be helped. But now the final course was done, and Annette sat useless, acting like a mouse for once. So, it was upon Shamaine to dig back into the strange and perfect beauty that was Quinn.

"So. Vivi's father? You took a break from your, what? Boyfriend? Fiancé? Matt, right?"

Quinn nodded guiltily.

"Then..." Shamaine wasn't dense. She could fill in the holes. But obviously what this woman needed was to let it all out. Shake the burden from her shoulders, take a deep breath, and know that there were worse things in life than getting lucky with two guys in the same fertility window.

At least, to Shamaine there were.

But Quinn was a funny duck. Probably why she fit in so well with the pipsqueaks on Apple Hill. A little uptight. A little perfect. A little Goody Two-Shoes. The sort of gal Shamaine was not—but the sort of gal Shamaine still admired. Even if from across the street.

At last, Quinn leveled her gaze on Shamaine, her jawline tight, her hands resting on the table. She took a deep breath. "Someone from town asked me on a date. Because I wasn't sure if I really *did* love Matt or if I needed to sow my oats, I said yes. It was supposed to be a test. A trial. He was doing it, too!" Her voice rattled.

"Who did you go out with?" Jude asked. All eyes turned to Jude. Of course, *Jude.* Jude who'd lived in Birch Harbor, where Matt was from. Where Quinn had been before. Did Jude know this secret person? Anticipation hung so heavily in the air Shamaine just about choked on it.

The pale green color returned to Quinn's face. She looked like she might be sick. Shamaine narrowed her eyes on Quinn. "You've got to say it. It's killing you, Quinn. No judgment here. Just say it."

"He was older," Quinn wobbled. "I was an aide at Birch Harbor High at the time. It was when I figured I might get my teaching credentials. Maybe I'd be a teacher." Her voice dropped, and she blinked. "He was the principal."

An audible gasp came from Jude. Shamaine's and the others' gazes ping-ponged from Jude to Quinn and back to Jude.

Jude *did* know this person. Quinn had been in Birch Harbor at the time. Nothing made sense to Shamaine.

CHAPTER 30—THE WOMAN

That ill-fated Thanksgiving, she'd arrived at Grandad's full of holiday cheer, but finding a missing woman there had, well, been nothing short of a shock.

The introduction had remained stiff, and the woman had known she'd have to leave. Right away. But first, she'd needed answers.

"Aren't you—?" she'd asked through nervous, rubbery lips.

Grandad had let out a cough, and his voice after that sounded younger. Happier. Less like that of the man she knew and more like that of a stranger. "Tippy and I have known each other since we were kids." He'd looked at Tippy with wonderment and affection, and the woman had felt suddenly as though this were *not* her home. As if she'd stumbled into someone else's Thanksgiving, and she'd been orphaned all over again.

They'd invited the woman in, but a haze of awkwardness had hung heavily in the house on Apple Hill Lane. The woman had known she'd have to leave.

But first, she'd needed those answers. "You're...alive?"

Tippy's smile had slipped. "In hiding. I've been camping out on Apple Hill Lane."

"Since when? *Why?* You're national news." The woman's gaze had flown to her grandfather then back to this ethereal stranger who wasn't strange, because her face was *everywhere* in Michigan. Had she been a child, she'd have been on a milk carton. But she wasn't a child, and she wasn't the same woman whose face had been advertised for years by then. She was older. Whiter. Wrinkled in new places.

Tippy had looked to Grandad for help.

He'd set his mouth in a line. "Kid," he said, his voice breaking over the vowel. "Remember what I told you about Nana?"

A sick feeling had coagulated the woman's blood, turning her gummy and shaky, and she nodded through the nausea.

"Tippy and I reconnected when Nana got bad. It was even Irma's folks who connected Irma and me with Tippy, in fact. Tippy worked there, at the hospital.

She helped Nana. We figured she could help, at least, but she made it worse. Everything just got *worse*."

"Okay…" the woman had replied, turning the words over in her mind, trying to make sense of everything.

"Months in—or more than a year—your Nana checked herself out, and she was bad. Real bad."

"It was the weekend when that happened," Tippy had interjected. "I was staying in Harbor Hills on the weekends."

The woman had shaken her head and frowned. "Why?"

They exchanged another look. Grandad had answered. "I wasn't honest with you, Kid. Or with your Nana. It wasn't that Nana came down because of any argument or anything. We did fight, sure. But she came down because I told her about Tippy 'n' me."

"Tippy and *you*?"

Like a pair of star-crossed teenagers, they'd fumbled for one another's hands. "Irma was so angry she wanted to *kill* Tippy." He'd half coughed, half laughed. "Heck, she wanted to kill *me*. I told Tippy to keep an eye out."

"One thing led to another. Your grandmother tried to attack me." Tippy's face had twisted into horror, but the woman hadn't bought it. Something had felt wrong. False. *Bad*. Tippy had taken a step closer to her. "It was self-defense."

"*What* was self-defense?"

Another step. "I pushed her away from me."

"Into a wall?"

"It wasn't a wall. I just—I was blinded with fear. I just pushed her back. She was acting crazy."

Grandad had added, "She *was* crazy."

"She was unhappy," the woman had tried to argue. "There's a difference."

"I've worked with patients like your grandmother before. They have unnatural strength. They can be moved to do terrible things. She was having a break. She was seeing red."

The woman had fallen back a step, shrinking away from this older stranger who *wasn't* a stranger to her grandfather. Who was a villain, so far as she could tell. Anger had risen in the woman right then, too. "She wasn't seeing red. She was seeing *you*," she'd spat back, straightening and leaning toward the thin, knobby cane of that now-found missing woman. Her gaze had flown to Grandad. "You had an affair? With *her*? And *hid* her? And..." A light bulb had flashed in her brain. "And *who* on earth is Carl? *You*? *You're* Carl Carlson?" What kind of an alias was *that*?

Grandad had scowled. "After what happened with Irma, I wanted to lie low. Everyone else was long gone, Kid. My folks 'n' hers. Brothers. Sisters. All of 'em. And, plus, with Tippy—" He'd hesitated. "With what happened between Tippy and Nana and all that confusion, it was best I just take on a different name. I'm no creative type, all right?"

She'd just shaken her head, all the more confused.

Grandad had huffed.

It was then that the woman had realized that only she was left to preserve any memory of Bernie. And one day, it would fall on her to bury him—or not. And it would fall on her to bury *Carl*, too.

Or not.

Grasping for the truth and for clarity, the woman had repeated her earlier claim. "You had an affair. *You* did all this?" Her stare had skipped from Tippy to Grandad and back again.

"It's not an affair," Tippy had reasoned. "It's love. We've always loved each other, but God had other plans."

"My family set the marriage with Irma," Grandad had added. "That didn't mean my feelings for my childhood sweetheart went away."

Tippy had nodded. "Irma probably had an affair of her own!"

"No," the woman had replied, shaking her head and a finger. "No, she wouldn't have done that. She was miserable. True. Miserable because of you two. And then you, what?" She'd swallowed hard. "Killed her?"

CHAPTER 31—BEVERLY

Everything made sense to Beverly. It made sense that Quinn and Jude seemed cold toward each other. Or, at least, that Quinn was reserved. Of course, Quinn was reserved with everyone. Did she even know Jude? Or Jude's history? Seemed highly unlikely.

But the whole of it did explain why a heavy cloud seemed to chase the poor woman. That even though her life appeared perfect, her smiles fled easily. Her anxiety grew out of her body, presenting itself to the world.

It made sense why Vivi and Quinn had had a falling out. Even if Vivi didn't know about her questionable parentage, she probably sensed it.

In this moment, Beverly realized that not a single one of them had had an easy life. And while it was easy for Beverly to claim she'd had it worse—and Shamaine a close second—it wasn't fair to compare. Beverly knew this, deep down. For every loss Beverly had experienced, each of her friends had experienced some pain, too.

In varying degrees, yes. But such was life, right? Such was God's will? Beverly shuddered at the very idea of a God. What God would drive Shamaine's son to do what he did? Would drive Tom to cheat? Would drive Quinn to the sorts of twitches and tics that made her a shaking mess half the time?

What God would take a child's life? *Kayla's* life?

Beverly didn't know. And what's more, she didn't want to know. Because knowing might strip her of her last threads of hope. Her last bit of will to live.

Her energy to move her whole life out of the house that her family had made was draining fast, and if she didn't push away from the table where a poor mother's drama spilled across like a felled glass of red wine... Beverly didn't know what she'd do.

She stood suddenly.

"I have to go."

"Go where?" Annette asked.

Beverly licked her lips and fumbled for her purse from the back of her chair. "I have to go. I can't—"

Shamaine grabbed Beverly's wrist. "Bev," she said calmly. "Wait. Just wait, okay?"

Beverly shook her head. "No, I—" She floundered

for the words, waving her hand erratically about the table. "It's too much. It's—too much."

"What's too much?" Annette broke in. "Quinn's affair?"

Silence took hold of all of them, and Beverly was left with only one thing to do. Sit back down.

"I didn't say that," Beverly managed.

"And I didn't have an affair," Quinn protested. "We were on a break."

But Annette didn't give her this out. "Okay, but that's what's got you all worked up. That you slept with someone other than your fiancé."

"I didn't—" Quinn's face streaked over in pain. "I didn't sleep with someone else while I was engaged." Now Quinn pushed up. "It wasn't like that!"

Jude curled her fingers around the table, her eyes searing. "I know what happened to you."

Everyone turned to Jude, and Quinn, like Beverly before her, lowered back down.

"What?" Quinn whispered. "What are you talking about?"

CHAPTER 32—THE WOMAN

"Oh, God." She was speaking now directly to the Lord above. Father Dan's presence beyond the wicker screen had faded into the background of the dark, wooden confessional booth.

"After we had it out, they tried to pretend everything was fine and that we could go on about Thanksgiving like a happy family. But we couldn't, of course. Still, I played along. I wasn't ready to give up my home. Not yet. Not after learning what I'd learned. I felt so miserably sad for Nana. It had hit me all at once, like a tidal wave of remorse. I'd hated her. She'd been so mean, but now I knew why, and I had done nothing to soften her hard life. I was swirling in my own pain, and I couldn't see that Nana was barely surviving. That she must have known all along about Bernie and Tippy.

She must have known they'd carried on next door together and started a new life. I was sickened by it all.

"We sat around his dining table while they pretended everything was fine. I didn't touch the turkey or the stuffing or anything. I just sat there as they cut their food into denture-worthy morsels and laughed and clinked their glasses.

"I was ready to leave. To leave and never look back. To find a new home, but then something happened. If you asked me, I'd have to say it was Nana, looking down on us from above. Exacting her revenge." A small, evil smile curled the side of the woman's face, but she flattened her mouth back into a line, shaking the compulsion to feel glad over such a horrible, horrible memory.

"Tippy seized up at the supper table, clutching her chest and staring ahead in this...*frozen panic*." The woman frowned hard. "Something was wrong with her. She was choking or maybe having a heart attack, and I didn't know what to do. I froze, too. Grandad tried to get to her, but his walker was in the way, and when he got up, he tripped over it or fell into it, or I don't know, but he didn't make it. And I just sat there, frightened, as Tippy slowly sort of leaned into the table then finally crumpled onto it.

"Grandad was a mess. He wanted to call an ambulance. I did, too. I...I looked for the portable phone while he patted her on the back and shook her body.

The house was such a mess. There was no phone anywhere. And by the time I gave up looking for the darn phone, we realized our situation. Tippy was a missing person. And if she died, she wouldn't be able to explain that she was there, at Grandad's, of her own volition. She wouldn't be able to explain that she'd run away to share a new life with a married man. Sure, she'd been in the property at 700, but only barely. And Grandad had the keys. Grandad could be implicated. *I* could have been implicated. We didn't know what in the world to do, but I did know one thing.

"I knew that secrets beget other secrets until you're so deep inside of them that you have to start life over again. And I knew that in order to start over, you have to run away.

"So that's what I did."

CHAPTER 33—JUDE

Jude set her jaw and gave Quinn a steely look. No, she hadn't known what had happened to Quinn. Not before tonight. It was only now that she put it all together.

But Jude did know what her husband had been up to. She always knew. It was never a secret. In fact, their relationship was quite a similar arrangement to that of Quinn and Matt's. Only the break lasted longer than a week. And only Gene had been allowed the *break* part.

"I know what happened to you because it happened to *me*." She said it clearly. Slowly. With as little emotion as she could convey—and that was quite a limited amount.

Ultimately, Jude had never loved Gene. She thought she had, sure. But to love someone, Jude figured three rules applied.

Firstly, you had to like them. And indeed, at first, Jude had really liked Gene. He was a winer and a diner. A charmer. Handsome and interesting. And the things they had in common. Oh! Not traveling, necessarily, no. But a love of education. A desire to give to children and expect nothing in return except for that warm feeling of sharing knowledge. Then there were the early days—when Jude was dead set against having children of her own. Gene had been happy to comply. Too happy, maybe. They'd agreed—the world was no place to raise a baby. Not in that day and age.

That was the second thing, though. The commonalities. In order to love someone, Jude had learned you had to share values. Not interests. Not hobbies. Not pizza toppings. Those were irrelevant when it came to the bigger moments in life. It occurred to her, just now, that she and Dean might share *no* interests, for all she knew. For all Jude knew, in fact, Dean liked pineapple on his pizza and stayed up all night watching Westerns. The only thing Jude really knew was that Dean was a Catholic and he put his faith ahead of quite a lot —maybe everything else. She wondered what other values he held. Did he believe in the marriage vow? In staying true? Did he believe in a contented life at home? Did he believe in eating well and exercising and in the healing power of cats?

Cats were important to Jude—laugh all you want. Without Liebchen, where would she be anyway?

The third thing you needed in order to love someone was the hardest thing. Knowing someone. *Really* knowing them. Not only knowing if you liked them or what their values were but the beyond. The deep beyond. Knowing someone's heart. Their mind. These were the things that eluded Jude. That she feared would always elude her.

And it turned out she was right. She hadn't known her family. Not really. And she hadn't known Gene. Not at all.

"Gene Carmichael is worse than people even know," Jude said at last.

The ladies stole furtive glances at each other.

Jude furrowed her eyebrows. Did they not know? Not know about Gene? What he did?

Why he was in *prison* as they spoke at this very moment?

Surely Quinn did. She'd have heard from Vivi or Matt or both.

"My ex-husband watched a man die years ago," Jude managed weakly.

Shamaine crossed her arms over her ample bosom and leaned back. "I do know about that case. A friend of mine is the DA who tried him. Eugene Carmichael, right?"

Jude nodded. "Gene. Right. Eugene."

Annette bristled in turn. "It's not a crime to watch someone die."

Beverly added darkly, "Unless you're the one who killed him."

Jude looked down at her lap and knit her fingers together. "It's a crime if you could help them and you don't."

"And," Quinn added now, squeezing Jude's hand beneath the table, "if you never confess."

CHAPTER 34—THE WOMAN

The woman would never forget what she learned about her family. She would never forget what she saw. What she *did*.

And so, she ran away.

Through the frost-lined streets of Michigan to the slushy shores of Lake Huron, the woman hopped on a ferry and returned to Heirloom Island.

But even there, a full town's-length away—a *Great Lake* away—from Harbor Hills, Apple Hill Lane felt much, *much* too close.

To try to shake off the shock, the woman spent the last few days of November engulfed in her work. Preparing for the Christmas recess.

December was about to hit, with all its alleged hope. Hope that the woman had learned belonged to other people.

But the woman had another kind of hope. She had Advent.

For the average family, the Christmas season was filled with gift shopping and tree trimming. For the St. Mary's live-in staff and students, it was filled with candle lighting and hymn singing. And while the poor little girls relegated to a boarding school may not have appreciated the somberness of Christ's coming, the woman cherished it as if *she* were the Blessed Virgin. As if *she* were swollen with a gift for all of humanity. As if with Christmas Day, the woman would finally birth the glory and happiness that she hadn't known since before her parents' deaths.

And even though the woman prized the yuletide and all it promised, she, too, grew bogged down in the solemnity.

She never could pin down from whence these doldrums came. Was it the dark wood of the pews? The stained glass through which the sun bled across the church in reds and purples? Or perhaps the hemorrhaging Christ, hanging miserably and sacrificially behind the altar?

Or maybe those selfsame hymns meant to spread Christmas cheer. Classic dirges like "Silent Night" and "O Holy Night." "Carol of the Bells"—that death knell of a melody. "Adeste Fideles." Why so somber, all those? Even the more modern songs like "Breath of Heaven" and "Mary, Did You Know?" echoed low and soberly through the narrow, shadowy halls of the girls' dormitory, turning the darkened wood paneling shades darker.

In the past, the woman had lived like one of the few nuns who served the church there on the island. She never left, really, even for the holidays. When other young faculty members sailed out the door on the last day of the semester, the woman hung around, oiling her desk and those of the students before carrying the rag and bottle to her own room in the main hall, where she oiled her own furniture and peeled splashes of dried wax from her purple Advent drape. Come evening, she'd drown herself in contraband—a romance novel replete with scandal and sex. The next morning, she'd arrive in the priest's office, scheduling herself for a confession before taking to the kitchen to start up the baking. Inevitably, a few of the more wayward girls would follow the smell of rising yeast and help her.

But now, here she was, spending Christmas at an educator's workshop. Her confession spoken and her penance given, the woman felt she could start fresh. Maybe this Christmastime would be a new time. Maybe she'd learn about a new job posting. Or she'd meet a new friend who'd invite her to spend New Year's Eve together. The woman could see it now— she'd be dressed in a sequined evening gown and a ridiculous, oversize faux-fur coat, snowflakes kissing her eyelashes as she chanted the countdown to a fresh start.

It was December 26, and the woman stood not in a sequined gown and fur coat but in a sensible maroon skirt and black tights, a black sweater buttoned up over a plain white button-down. Black clogs on her feet. She looked every bit the part of a Catholic schoolmarm. Even if she was younger and prettier and a fan of smut. Christmas music—jaunty and light—clanged over the sound system in the conference room at the Henry Ford Museum.

The woman eyed an empty table at the back of the room and beelined toward it.

But she'd only just sat down when a man's deep voice boomed over the Christmas music. "Let's all move up a little closer, shall we? No hiding!" The crowd buzzed with polite laughter, and it was then that the woman realized he was directing his announcement at her. Frazzled and goosebumpy now, she wobbled up from the safety of that far-back seat and made her way to a table along the edge, near a midroom exit, where only two others now sat.

And there she felt safe. Safe from ridicule. Safe from humiliation. Safe from the presenter—that charismatic administrator from some little lakeside district the woman hadn't quite caught.

The conference droned on for the better half of a wintry week, and by its end, the woman had made no new friends, been invited to no New Year's Eve parties, and learned no new things that might catapult her to some greater status than a measly ol' schoolteacher.

But on the last day, her luck changed.

On the last day, the presenter—the same one who had shamed her for tucking herself far away from the others—found her. And he introduced himself. And it turned out they had something in common, the woman and that administrator. Something that felt safe. Familiar. *Good.*

They lived very close to each other.

She on Heirloom Island. And he just a stone's throw away. In the quaint, charming, sparkling, nearby community of Birch Harbor.

CHAPTER 35—QUINN

Quinn, too, was familiar with Jude's ex-husband's unfortunate series of events. Vivi was a gossip machine, and any juicy tidbit like what had happened back in Birch Harbor had quickly made the rounds among locals—even the younger set, such as Vivi's friend group.

"What Gene did, says nothing about you," Quinn pointed out to Jude. "You have to let that go."

"It's not only what he did to that man," Jude replied ominously, darkly. "It's what he did to me."

Quinn felt her throat close up. To hear that the good Gene Carmichael, silver-haired fox and charming sixty-something, could have done something to his *wife* would be...welcome? Surprising? Expected? Quinn felt desperate, suddenly. Desperate for the truth. Quinn wanted Jude to tell the truth. She needed Jude to tell the truth. To say that Gene was the problem. Not Jude.

Not Quinn.

Not the twenty-something who'd been taken in by a forty-something with a great boat and mystery money and an aura of sex appeal and promise.

"Gene stepped out on me. Without my consent. He did a lot of things without my consent."

"I consented," Quinn acknowledged, her voice low. "It was—out of character for me. I didn't know what I wanted, but I knew things with Matt were weird. He wasn't all in. I needed to protect myself, I guess?"

"From the truth?" Shamaine asked.

Quinn frowned at her.

Shamaine pursed her lips. "Matt gave you lip service. His heart was somewhere else, and you knew it."

Quinn turned defensive. "He said he loved me."

"You saw other people, though. You saw Gene, who was married." Beverly said all this simply, like she was reviewing the facts in an easy court case. Like feelings weren't attached. Deep feelings.

Quinn gave Jude a pleading look. "I didn't know—"

But Jude's face was as open and soft as Quinn had ever seen it. "If it were a slight against me—an offense, I mean—I'd forgive you." Her lips lifted into a smile.

"But it wasn't. It wasn't about me. It wasn't even about Gene. It was about you."

"But it became something about my daughter, too." Quinn felt a heave coming up. To think—Gene Carmichael, convicted felon and now an old man, could be Vivi's dad. It was too much. It was too much to take, and Quinn *couldn't* take it, and the bile was rising in her throat and—

"Quinn," Jude broke the tension with the clean cut of her name.

Quinn looked at her.

"Gene isn't Vivi's father."

A collection of gasps sucked the air clear off the table as all eyes turned on Jude.

Quinn found her voice, weak though it may have been. "What?"

"He had a procedure. He couldn't possibly be Vivi's father."

~

EVEN AFTER TEARS of happiness and a burst of inappropriate giggles—giggles of relief—Quinn still had to let out all of the angst and pain inside.

Once the conversation naturally moved away, Quinn excused herself to the restroom, where she got sick until her belly was empty, her throat was raw, and her eyes stung from rubbing off the tear-streaked makeup. Before long, someone joined her in there. Her eyes still squeezed shut, she started back for a stall, to hide, but the woman's voice came again.

"You aren't alone, Quinn."

Quinn swiveled. Annette stood there; she looked... broken somehow. Different. Changed.

Unsure exactly what she meant, Quinn just shrugged.

"You're not the first woman to question the paternity of her child. You're not the first woman to have regrets."

"Maybe not," Quinn replied. "But it's not who I am. It's...not who I was supposed to be, either. A slut—"

"You're human," Annette replied. "You still deserve love."

"Love?" Quinn could almost laugh. "Who could even *like* a human—a woman—like me? I don't even like me." It was true. It was the plain truth, really. It was the thing Quinn had run from all her life. The thing she was compelled toward but from which she ran.

"I like you." Annette took a tentative step toward Quinn. It was foolish. The two of them in the bathroom like teenagers at high school, escaping reality in a cloud of drama. All that was missing was the thick smell of CoverGirl compacts and an aerosol can of Rave.

Quinn gave Annette a look. "Even now? Now that you know who I really am?"

"I like you even *more* now that I know who you really are. You're not perfect. Frankly, it's a relief."

They laughed and returned their gazes to one another. "I'm like a token friend—the only person you know with such a sordid past."

Annette's eyes welled up, and Quinn realized that her smile had been plastered and her laughter high and hollow. Now, she was full on crying and shaking her head and running the backs of her hands across her face just as Quinn had mere minutes before.

"Annette?"

Annette looked at Quinn. "Let's just say you're not the only one with a sordid past."

Quinn gave her a hard look. A serious look. A look to say, *No. You're better than that, Annette. You're better than me.*

But then what were friends if they were perfect? Better than? More pristine and angelic and sin-free? Angels, probably. And Quinn knew Annette was no angel.

In fact, that's *why* they were friends.

"I know what happened to Temperance Temper. I've always known."

CHAPTER 36—THE WOMAN

It wasn't until later, on a particularly difficult weekend, that the woman finally returned to Apple Hill Lane.

She'd married that man—that administrator from Birch Harbor—and they'd started their life together, but it was never easy. Like most men, she came to realize, his eye wandered. Sometimes far, too. Sometimes, *he* even wandered, taking his boat and drifting across Lake Huron and up and down the shores of the small towns peppering that grassy Michigan coastline.

It was on one such weekend, almost a year since she'd met him, when her husband was gone, that the woman felt especially stir-crazy. She didn't call ahead. No point.

Christmas was coming, and at the very least, the woman would do some light shopping on Main Street.

Harbor Hills had a great bakery and a reasonably priced clothing boutique. Wouldn't the ladies back at St. Mary's each enjoy a new scarf? She could afford it easily, and it would mean so much. Or, if not scarves, then pies. As she was still working there, at the school, maybe the woman would even organize a holiday party.

And, of course, there was her husband to shop for. He deserved something nice. Something he couldn't get at any of his ports of call. Something that would tie him to her a little more firmly than that hollow vow they'd recited hurriedly in church one Saturday morning, when no one else was around.

Something in the woman told her that if she returned to the house on Apple Hill Lane, just for a moment, maybe she'd find the peace she needed to push ahead with this new life. Maybe a different strength. One that she hadn't known she had. Maybe she'd go so far as to make things right, even.

At the very least, she could find out what locals had made of the case of the missing Temperance Temper.

But when the woman arrived there, at 696, the chill in the air was more powerful than something that could be merely weather related. It indicated a change. Something big. Something cold. The stacks of boxes and piles of belongings had now encroached on every last corner of the porch and all along the front of the garage, creeping even farther down toward the street.

The grass was so overgrown and the trees so poorly tended, that one could scarcely make out the house beyond all that weedy green mixed together with a recent falling of snow.

Even up against a clear hoard, the woman made her way to the front door and knocked hard.

No response. No creaking cane from within. No footsteps. Wind whipped through the porch, causing the woman to twist to shield herself from such cold. As she turned her face away and down the street, she saw other changes, too. Signs. Poking out here and there at what used to be rentals. Three of them. One at the house at the end of the cul-de-sac. One at the house across the street, the lone house that sat opposite 696. And one at the house that should belong to *her*. To the woman. The house promised to her by her grandfather.

For-sale signs.

And where was the one next door? At the house where Temperance had her run-in with Nana?

She banged a fist on the door again. Still no response.

The woman backed away from the house and peered up into the windows before glancing around herself. At last, anger boiling up inside, she held her hands to her mouth and hollered loudly through the swirling cold air. "Grandad!"

Nothing.

"Grandad!"

Again, nothing.

Seething, she shook her head and decided *fine*. She'd march right over there and see for herself.

And march, she did. All the way down the hill to the house that rightfully belonged to her. The one he had *promised* her. The one she had saved in her heart as a back-up plan. Just in case...

Just in case things with her new husband didn't go swimmingly. Or, maybe, in case they *did*. Who knew where life might go, and it wasn't such a bad idea to save Apple Hill for something. Especially if it wasn't 696.

But as she marched down there, she had the funny feeling of someone watching her.

"I'm right here." Grandad appeared at the backyard gate of the house next to his. The one that sat between 700—her heirloom property with the for-sale sign —and 696.

The woman glared at him. "You're selling it?"

"I figured you were gone for good." His face filled with spite. For the first time, perhaps, there was no kindness to be seen in Grandad's face. Nothing at all except the misery that had poked out in just bits and pieces before. As though there was nothing left for him in life. Not the woman's holiday visits. Not Nana. And not Tippy.

"I'm not." The woman, emboldened by this change

in him—this inflamed crotchetiness—strode up to where he leaned against the backyard gate of the neighbor house. "I'm back. I—want that house." She didn't say that, actually, she *needed* that house.

But as she neared him, a strangeness materialized. Gone was his walker. Gone was his wheezing. Instead —and although he leaned heavily into the fence—his face was mottled in dirt and grime. He looked younger somehow. Tired. Worn out. But younger. At the edges of the muddy earth streaked over his cheeks, a redness bloomed. Not strawberry-nose red or alcoholic red. The red from working hard. From doing something.

She cocked her head. "Grandad, what are you doing back there?"

CHAPTER 37—ANNETTE

Annette was tired of the secret. It had hung so heavily in her heart and for so long that if she didn't let it out for the world to know, then she might just sink into the earth from the very weight.

By the time Annette had dragged Quinn back to the table, where she intended to share everything with everyone, it was clear their time at the Dorgendorf was up. Dessert had finished. Drinks were emptied. Waiters were loitering and stealing discreet glances at wristwatches they didn't wear.

Outside, in the nippy air, Annette knew she had moments to explain what she had meant. Quinn might be her closest friend these days, but it wouldn't feel right until Annette told *everyone*. But she had only moments now. Moments until each of them had tucked away into her own car, plump and content from their wintry meal and sweet pie.

"Wait," she said just as the ladies looked like they were about to disperse.

Everyone turned, obedient to their friend. "What is it, Annette?" Shamaine asked, folding her arms. "It's cold as a witch's kiss out here."

Annette shared a look with Quinn, who nodded her on encouragingly. "Sorry. Um. I have to tell you all something. I have to."

"It *is* really cold," Elora complained.

"What is it?" Beverly asked, looking more earnest than the others.

Annette exchanged a look with Quinn. Unreadable but soft. Quinn's mouth shaped in an arc, her eyebrows knitted together. Then, as though Quinn could read Annette's very thoughts, she spoke up. "How about we have a nightcap at my place?"

∾

It hadn't been hard to round up the troops in Quinn's living room. With a roaring fire, hot cocoa, popcorn, and Elora's kids duly entertained by Vivi and Elijah in the den, it was *nice*. Comfortable. The perfect opportunity for Annette to come clean.

She pushed her sweater sleeves up and leaned forward, lacing her fingers together around her knees. And then, she confessed.

CHAPTER 38—THE WOMAN

Once the woman was right next to Grandad at the neighbor's backyard gate, she didn't need to ask him what he'd been doing. It was clear as day.

He'd been digging. How—she didn't know. The ground was starting to freeze. Maybe it was already frozen.

Bewildered, she pressed him for details, anyway. "You're digging a garden? It's *snowing*."

He didn't answer. He just followed her gaze to where his work had been—a muddy, frosty lump of earth at the far-right corner of the yard. Clear as day. And a garden it might have been. A garden or another of those morbid backyard burial sites for which the Carlson clan displayed such a bizarre fondness. She frowned and her gaze flew back to him. "No. You didn't.

Grandad." Each word came out staccato. Stilted. Interrupted by what whirred in her mind.

That Grandad hadn't taken care of things yet—horrifyingly and stupidly. In winter, the ground would be much harder to break.

It was clear now that he wasn't planting flowers.

She felt herself grow cold beneath her coat, under her knit hat. Her mittens. Ice cold. She looked her grandfather directly in the eye. "It's *her*."

Grandad's face glowed red, and he started up with the wheezing. "What in the *hell* did you *think* I was going to do, Kid?" Spittle flung out between his lips. He was as angry as she'd ever seen anyone. Scary mad, even. He clutched his hand to his heart. "What in the *hell* did you think?" His eyes bulged.

"Grandad, it's *okay*," she assured, stepping up to where he was at the gate and gripping his mud-encrusted knuckles. "Whatever you did, it's okay. It'll be fine." She looked beyond him to the mottled pile. She was complicit. Totally. An accessory. A criminal. A felon. Everything bad in the world. But then another thought occurred to her. The for-sale sign next door. "But—why are you selling the house? The one you promised me?"

"Can't sell this one now," he grunted, hooking a thumb toward the shallow tomb.

"Why didn't you bury her in *your* yard? Or in the family lot?"

"Running out of room over there. Too many others." He sniffed and snorted, and his face cleared of the deep red flush, somewhat.

"But *your* backyard? It's private."

"It'd connect me."

He was making no sense. Garbled jumbo. That's all he had to offer by way of explanation. "You own this entire block. Half of Crabtree Court—or whatever it's called—belongs to you. You're connected regardless."

But she was arguing with someone who didn't have all his marbles. Someone old and decrepit who'd just endured who knew how many minutes or hours of heavy manual labor that he had no business enduring. And even more than that, she was arguing with a man who had a broken heart.

A man the woman didn't know.

Didn't want to know.

"Well, I'm selling 'em all off anyway, so I'm not connected. There now. Ya see? I've got the right idea." He said it for his own benefit as much as for hers.

"You're selling my house, too?"

"I got to, Kid." He looked sad about it but only just. "I got to sell it or else I'm connected."

"You're connected, anyway, Grandad," she whispered, her voice hoarse.

He waved her off. "Just go, will ya?"

Affronted, she frowned. "What?"

"Just get the hell outta here. I'm done with it. With

everything and everyone!" His voice rose up into a crescendo. She took a step back, panicked. Here she was, married to a man she just barely trusted. No living kin except for her grandfather, who was losing his mind just as he'd lost the last love of his life.

"Don't sell it, please," she begged now, glancing back to the beautiful brick house with the fateful pony wall. The house that now meant so much to her. The house she thought she might just move into one day.

The house where she might raise a baby. Grow her family. Celebrate birthdays and dole out Halloween candy and welcome Christmas morning.

But instead, the old man whom the woman had grown to love so dearly, despite *everything*, snarled at her one final time. "You ruined everything, Kid. If *you* hadn'ta come 'long Irma and I'da divorced and Tippy 'n' I'da been together in the light of day. I'da called an ambulance. It'da been no big secret, but *you* and your folks had to go and ruin everything. Now here you are, asking me for handouts and ruining Christmas, too. Just like that house." He pointed to the pretty white house. "Where Tippy 'n' me had to handle Nana that ol' Christmas."

Tears stung the woman's eyes, and she was shell-shocked at what her grandfather was saying. At what he thought of her and her mom and dad and the tragedy that was her life.

When she turned back, ready to fight one last time

—to *try* one last time—he stabbed his stumpy, gnarled finger at the house again. "The house," he growled, "that ruined Christmas. The house that ruined my life!"

~

SHE DROVE BACK to Birch Harbor in sullen silence. On one hand, none of what Grandad had said made sense.

But on the other, all of it did. She could see clearly now what he really was, and he wasn't her grandfather. He wasn't Nana's husband. Maybe not even her mother's father. Not in the real sense of the word. He was only a man with a confused heart and a grudge against the world. A man who kept a missing woman hidden and his own kin cut off.

By the time the woman got home, her husband had returned, too. He wanted to know what she'd been up to all day. Where had she been?

"Christmas shopping," she lied plainly.

"Oh yeah?" he asked. "Speaking of Christmas gifts, what does my beautiful new bride want for Christmas?"

She looked thoughtfully at him, and an idea hit her like a ton of fireplace bricks. "A second home," she replied.

Her husband laughed at first, but at length, he ran his hand across his mouth and turned serious. "And just where in the world would you like to own a second home?"

Forcing back the sobs and pain of the last several decades of her life, the woman felt like a girl again. Like she was at the crossroads between hope and disappointment. Still, she replied, "Somewhere on a hill full of apples."

CHAPTER 39—SHAMAINE

Shamaine had yet to be retained here in Harbor Hills. And not all of the women knew she still had her Michigan license. That she could still be helpful to them, should any of them need it. And it seemed like at least one of them would.

She had her eye on Quinn, who was probably ready to sue Gene Carmichael for all he was worth— too bad, though. You couldn't squeeze water from a stone on that one. He turned broke just as soon as the DA proceeded with charges.

Then there was Elora and Tad. What a winner. She could really take it to him if she had a mind to. But then, if all Shamaine had to contribute to Harbor Hills was a list of lawsuits against the crummy men of her hometown, was she *really* helping? Or was there another way to be a force for good? Could she help these women without adding to a backlog of court appointments and disappointing outcomes?

Maybe.

But then there was Annette, who—if her admission that she had a dark, deep secret was valid—might *actually* need legal counsel. For once in her life, Shamaine realized that there was only one thing she could do.

One thing she *should* do.

One thing she should have done years ago with her son. The thing she didn't do.

Listen.

So, that's what she did. She leaned back, closed her mouth, and *listened*.

CHAPTER 40—BEVERLY

Beverly had so much to do. Pack. Move houses. Call Darry. She gave her head a silly shake. Call *Darry*? That was not a priority.

No.

But what was, was being there for these women. These women who'd surrounded her in love and hot dinners—in sympathy and kindness in a time she'd needed it. And beyond that, too. In a promise of indefinite support.

That evening, Beverly *had* put away thoughts about work—about the gala she ought to be planning. About her new column and the questions people had for her every single day. The emails. The letters that came in. She put thoughts away about Vivi and Elijah and their well-meaning hunt for a woman Beverly had started to believe didn't exist.

Until now. A hunch throttled her stomach, twisting her dinner and exciting her like she'd gotten a fresh lead on a hot story. Something told Beverly that whatever Annette had to say was *big*.

"What is it, Annette?" she pressed.

Everyone's breath hitched, and even Vivi appeared in the doorway that connected the den to the living room.

"Years ago, when Roman's parents initially connected us with a rental agent here in town, we looked at a few houses first. Right? I mean, we knew we wanted to be here. We agreed about that. It was a great place to raise kids. Safe. You know?"

Beverly nodded because she'd had the same exact conversation with Tom. She'd implored him. *Please. I grew up here.* That should have been evidence enough that Harbor Hills was worthy. But what Beverly didn't know back then, and what she didn't know today, was that she only *really knew* of the Harbor Hills of her youth and of her own experience. Not the before. Not even the during.

But now, she would know *the after*. She would know what would happen to her in the wake of her daughter's death. Her husband's infidelity. His death, too. She would know what would become of a woman whose world was sucked out from around her, leaving her to spin like a dervish and melt and dissolve and crumble in the shell of what was once her happy, safe *home*.

"They got in touch with a local property owner," Annette went on tentatively. "Carlson. Roman's family knew of him because he'd been renting out houses that he owned. Here. Back then, Crabtree Court was just taking shape. Carlson must have sold off land here, but I remember them saying he seemed frantic. Frantic to sell."

Beverly easily remembered her own mother discussing the growth of Harbor Hills. She was just returning home, having convinced Tom that Crabtree Court, the new development—or relatively new development—was the *place* to be. The place to raise a family. Better than where she'd grown up, even. Tom had always preferred to live out in the woods due to some half-hearted Thoreauvian yearning.

"At the time," Annette continued, "we were feeling a little desperate. House prices were starting to climb—it was right before the bubble—and our options seemed so limited. In fact, *three* of the homes on this street had just sold. The Carlson family had listed them, and they'd gone in a flash. So, Roman's mom went to the property manager for the Carlson family and asked about the remaining properties on Apple Hill Lane."

"The remaining properties?" Jude interjected. "How did you know there *were* remaining properties?"

"Well, we didn't. We just knew there were still a couple of houses on the street that sat vacant. At least, they *looked* vacant. One had even had a for-sale sign at one point, my mother-in-law had said. I remember, because she told me that as soon as that house had hit the market, it had sold. It was all murky then, and it's even murkier now that I'm trying to recall. It's been so many years."

It was Vivi, at the doorway, who interrupted them. "Does this have something to do with Temperance Temper?"

Beverly swallowed hard. Memories were flooding back. Memories of when she covered the story for the first time. How it went nowhere. How even the Temper family didn't want to talk about it. Claimed they knew *nothing.* At the time, Beverly, a young upstart reporter, hadn't known to question that. At the time, she hadn't known what a mother's love could do. That it could move mountains. That it could track kidnappers and lift vehicles and concoct elaborate lies if it meant those lies might save the mother's child.

"Oh my heavens," Beverly whispered at the realization. It had already been implanted in her brain—Vivi and Elijah had put it there. A theory. Loose and rough and unlikely.

And all the same, it made perfect sense.

"I know how you know what happened to Temperance Temper." She looked at Annette, waves of nausea rocking her forward. "She's the skeleton in your backyard."

CHAPTER 41—JUDE

Elora was the first to gasp. And naturally so. After all, it was she who lived in the house where the skeleton had recently been found.

However, it was Jude who felt sick. She felt *sick* as sin. She felt like she'd felt all those years ago when she, just like Annette now, had to fess up to a truth that wasn't *really* hers but that still somehow defined her.

Even so, Jude remained silent. She let Elora, instead, dig at Annette's so-called truth. "You knew there was a missing woman buried on your property? And you...you still bought the house?"

Annette held up a finger as she took a slow sip of her cocoa. "Rented. At first. And no—I didn't know. Not at first. All we knew was that the property owner said there were family plots in the area."

"This is *so* confusing," Vivi complained, leaving Eli

to watch Elora's kids and joining the other women in the living room. She sank into the seat next to her mom. "I mean...I *figured* it was Tippy. The skeleton. It was obvious. But you *knew*? And you never said?"

Annette was quiet for a beat. "I'm starting to regret it."

"It's not her fault," Jude added, but her remark was swept up in a cacophony of chatter and contention over what Annette should have done, why she should have done it, how, and so forth.

It was Shamaine, however, who called them back to order with one shrill whistle through her fingers. "Let's listen to her story, for goodness' sake. Shall we?" Shamaine staved off an eyeroll, quite obviously, then gave the floor back to Annette.

"There's not much to the story, admittedly. When we moved in, we had a dog. It sort of happened like with Sadie, actually. But Leroy was his name. He was a mutt, and he was a great dog. Before we moved here, I'd never known him to dig. Ever. He was just a really good dog. Then, the day we moved in, he went out to relieve himself and never came back in.

"Roman was in Detroit at a convention. He and his parents and brother had already gotten us moved in, it was just a matter of Leroy and me driving to town and unpacking. I was six months pregnant and home alone. So I was in the kitchen, unpacking our wedding china, and I called for Leroy, but he didn't hear me. Or maybe ignored me. I don't know, but I wasn't scared. I figured Leroy was maybe lost or confused. I went out to fetch him, and he wouldn't come. I could see that Leroy was in the far corner, digging something up. I didn't think twice about it until, again, the dog just would not come. So I ventured out there, and sure enough, I could see he was working up a rug or a blanket from under the soil. I gave it a tug, and the whole thing slid out of the earth. It couldn't have been all that old, but I could also see that it was meant to cover something. The way it had been lying. Leroy kept at it, and that was when I knew."

"Knew what?" Jude cried.

"It was the family plot. The grave that the property owner had disclosed."

"Did anything...*you know*...come *up*?" Beverly asked.

Annette shook her head. "It was writhing in bugs. I was fairly disgusted, frankly. I pulled the blanket out of the ground and tossed it aside then dragged the dog back in. I never let him out again, and once Roman returned home, I told him we needed to do something about it. That there was an infestation or something."

"You didn't tell Roman it was a *body* under there? Remains?" Quinn asked gently.

Shrugging, Annette replied, "I mean, what did it matter? I figured if he got weird about it, we might have to involve authorities or something. Since the grave wasn't marked, you know. And if we involved authorities, maybe then we couldn't buy the place. And I was desperate to live there."

Jude considered all of this and looked at Elora, who'd remained quiet as a mouse, as always. Curiosity struck Jude, though, and she spoke up. "Elora, why did you and Tad want to buy on Apple Hill?"

"It's the best street in Crabtree Court. Plus, we needed a bigger house. And Tad said he knew the people on the street."

At this, Annette bristled. "We didn't know Tad."

"Technically we did," Vivi chimed in. With a Christmas cartoon blaring on the TV in the den, Eli had meandered out and hovered nearby, too. He nodded urgently.

"Everyone knew about Mr. Beckett."

Elora paled. "Oh."

"Not like that—" Vivi added, but she was too slow. The humiliation had already colored Elora's cheeks and neck.

"It's actually how Tad and I met, too." She said this so quietly that Jude wasn't sure she'd heard right.

"What?" Beverly asked her to repeat herself. Elora did, and there was a new scuffle. A new drama. Something to overshadow the current scandal of Annette knowing about a random dead body buried in her backyard. Now, it appeared, the dead body was little more than an inconvenience. A nuisance. And the group had found a new, juicier morsel to feast over. Elora's courtship with Tad Beckett, local scoundrel.

Jude was disgusted. Elora started moaning and groaning that it was *all her fault* and *if she hadn't validated Tad's preferences for younger girls by dating him when he was her teacher, then he'd have never victimized more girls.* And *at the very least she never should have married him and had children.* And *what if their kids turn out like Tad?*

Jude snapped. "You're joking," she spat, shaking her head at Elora, then at Annette and Quinn and Beverly and Shamaine, skipping over Vivi and Elijah, who were there only for the show. The spectacle. Nothing more. Not true connection. Just nosiness. "You're all joking. You think you know guilt." She snorted a scornful laugh. "You know *grief*. Not guilt." The others, stunned, just sat and listened to her, and so Jude shone. She took her moment, and she let it all out.

Once and for all.

CHAPTER 42—THE WOMAN

The woman stared at the others, taking in the whole of each and every last one of them. Their faces, their sweaters, the mugs of hot cocoa they clutched in anticipation of what may come next.

Mostly, she wondered what it would be like, from here on out. Now that every last one of them had come clean about her checkered history. Her insidious past. Would they go on to enjoy a merry holiday season? A festive gala, three days' worth of Christmas events culminating in the perfect floating Christmas supper? Would Elora make ends meet now that she was downsizing into Beverly's house? Would Annette's future pay off, too? And what about Quinn and Beverly and Jude and their brokenness? Would Christmas fix them?

Or would it all end today?

Suddenly, getting this far in life—far enough to sit with a living room full of girlfriends and share secrets and sip cocoa and munch popcorn—felt like a fantasy. A television show, even. Something bored housewives watched with tepid interest, at first, only to grow in their fascination over the not-so-incredible lives of the ladies down the street.

The woman had already lived a lifetime to get here, and it felt like, in a way, a happy ending. Even with her fledgling romance—if she could call it that—the true love she now nurtured had nothing to do with a certain someone. It had to do with the women who lived on her very own street, in her very own home-town. If she could call Harbor Hills *that*. Now Christmas was coming, and the woman wondered if *this* would be the one. The Christmas that saved all those Christmases of the past. The broken ones. The ones that ended in crushing disappointment and sobs against the backdrop of those yuletide hymns of yore, with their echoing chants and moody instrumentals.

But if this were to be the good Christmas, which it very well might, how could they possibly arrive there? The woman didn't know.

And then her eye caught on something. Something she'd never noticed before.

She wouldn't have seen it, either, if it weren't for the

white sweater that Vivi wore. Over top of that, just at the hollow of where the teenager's collarbones slid in together, sat the charm. The piece of the woman's past. The thing that she'd lost so long ago that she'd started to forget what it meant to her.

That, despite it all, she *did* have a family. A family who loved her. And so, if these friends sitting 'round weren't enough—couldn't love her enough, or if she couldn't love them enough—there once had been a mother and father who had. Who loved the woman who was once a girl who became an orphan and landed on Apple Hill Lane.

"Vivi," she said. "Where did you find that?" She pointed a shaky, holly-berry-red-painted nail directly at the bottom of a burnished silver chain on this neighbor girl's chest. At a silver pendant in the shape of the letter *B*.

The others looked at the teenager, at the silver *B* she now pinched in her fingers. "In my house?" she replied, glancing first at her mother then at Eli. It felt cruel, her visual discovery, but then that was the woman's life, was it not? A string of little cruelties, all culminating in this one moment. This one moment of recognition and flashback to the life before. The life that *began* there, on the hill without apples on Apple Hill Lane.

Vivi's eyes grew wide, with compassion or realization. They grew wide at the woman who had already explained herself to them. Who'd told them everything, from start to finish. The woman who once was an orphan. The woman who once was Judith Banks.

Judy.

Jude.

CHAPTER 43—BEVERLY

I n the weeks between Jude's confession and Christmas, things on Apple Hill Lane were hectic, to say the least.

Directly after Jude revealed that Annette's hunch was right—it was Temperance Temper buried in Elora's backyard—Vivi and Eli flew into action, prepared to take their newest findings to the police or something. But their excitement was mitigated by the rational minds of the women who'd huddled together at Quinn's house.

Surprisingly, it was Beverly who first sprang into action. As if she'd been lying dormant for the past year, she suddenly had all the answers. This actually made sense, because it was Beverly who knew how small-town news worked, and it was vital to get ahead of the story. Lawyer Jude up. Annette, too, for that matter. Then Beverly, with Forrest's oversight, would run a quick piece at the bottom half of the front page.

MISSING WOMAN FOUND, Laid to Rest with Family

YEARS AGO, Birch Harbor Native Temperance "Tippy" Temper went missing from her place of employment in Detroit. Local lore placed her in the greater southwestern Lake Huron area. Indeed, a recent investigation reveals that she passed of natural causes soon after her disappearance. Additionally, authorities have come to the conclusion that she was loved and buried by a close, elderly friend who suffered from dementia. Judith Carmichael, a relative of the man responsible for the burial, has assumed all costs associated with the investigation and reinterment of the remains of Ms. Temper. No family members exist to press civil charges, but community members have asked that anyone who wishes to remember Tippy do so by donating to their local mental health charity.

BEVERLY'S DECISION TO use Jude's married name was intentional, of course. And not quite unethical. She reasoned that it wasn't the current Jude who'd turned a cheek on the missing woman. It was the broken Judith, with the dead parents and the lost pendant and the grandparents with problems so big they could never have shown their granddaughter the love she deserved. No, that wasn't the Jude who now lived in 700 Apple Hill. Who was a friend to every woman on the street and teacher to half the town's high school students. The woman who cared about Harbor Hills. About others. The woman who held fast to her faith and her hope despite all odds.

Above that article? None other than the most inspirational bit of news to cross the desk of the *Herald* in as many years as Tippy had been missing.

RESIDENTS OF APPLE *Hill Lane to Host Holiday Gala with Meaning*

COME PAY *your respects to the memory of the Carlson family and Tippy Temper by lighting a candle and offering a prayer. Donations will go toward the resettlement of the Carlson family cemetery to a proper, formal site at the Harbor Hills Cemetery on Schoolhouse Street.*

After, please join the town council, the Crabtree Court HOA, and other officials as we enjoy a holiday feast fit for the Ghost of Christmas Present. Don't miss Harbor Hills' three-day Christmas extravaganza, culminating in a floating Christmas supper on Apple Hill Lane, where guests will move from house to house for each course, spreading out the festivities across the quaint, suburban cul-de-sac.

CHAPTER 44—BEVERLY

Beverly gave herself a final inspection in the bathroom mirror. In a white knit sweater, dark-wash jeans, and brown boots, she looked and felt as fresh and put-together as she possibly could, for what might have otherwise been a difficult evening. All of December had been difficult, no doubt. But having the gala to look forward to and prepare for had been instrumental in keeping her afloat.

The gala *and* Darry's companionship. No, they weren't dating. It was way too soon for that. But there was something there between them that was helping to thaw her frozen heart. That's why Beverly had asked him to help host her part of the gala—holiday beverages in the cottage at the corner of Dogwood and Crabtree—her new home. It was stop one of four for the highly anticipated evening of celebration.

The whole thing was all very organized, thanks to Annette's careful planning and many people's help. Not the least of which were the menfolk. Darry, Forrest, Dean, Roman, and Eli had spent every spare moment moving Beverly to Annette's cottage, Annette back to her old house, and Elora into Beverly's house. The result was nothing short of magic, in such a short time span. And yet, it worked out for the best because now, three of them had that brand-new house look for the floating dinner party.

Beverly's assignment was simple: drinks in the cottage for starters—this way people swept in and out of Beverly's small home quickly, but long enough for her to snap some photos for the write-up she'd do.

She leaned closer to the mirror and applied a neat layer of red lipstick. Couldn't hurt to add a touch of color, after all.

A knock came at the front door.

Darry, Beverly's special cohost. She smacked her lips and capped her lipstick, then strode to the front door, opening it to find that he nearly matched her in dark denim and a crisp white button-up with a Christmas tie. They each glanced down at their own outfits, laughing at the coincidence.

Then, Darry lifted a neatly wrapped box, brown

paper packaging tied up with red string. He passed it to her. "Merry Christmas, Beverly."

She clicked her tongue. "You really shouldn't have." Gifts had been far down on her list of priorities that year. Christmas shopping reminded her almost exclusively of Kayla. It felt improbable that Beverly could possibly ever give anyone a wrapped present again. Or even receive one. Nothing would compare to the many special gifts she'd presented her daughter, nor would any gift ever hold a candle to the many special gifts Kayla had presented her mother.

Never again would Beverly receive a gift as great as the gift of sixteen years with her sweet, smart, beautiful, perfect daughter.

About ready to wave him off and decide she couldn't do this, Beverly shook her head. She couldn't host. Couldn't pretend. But Darry took a step closer. "It's small. It...reminded me of you."

What could possibly remind him of me? Beverly wondered internally. Her cynical heart tightened in her chest, but she reluctantly took the package and untied the string, winding it around her hand before lifting the simple rectangles of tape at each side. The box within was plain, white. Inside of it, white tissue paper, light as newly fallen snow. Tucked neatly within was a cashmere scarf the color of the sky. Ethereal and beautiful.

And heartbreakingly perfect.

"Here," Darry said, his tone hushed and his movement delicate. He took the box and lifted the impossibly soft scarf to reveal a second item. A white ceramic Christmas ornament in a shape initially indiscernible. Darry held it so she could read an inscription on the back.

Kayla Castle
   Her Mother's Christmas Angel

OF COURSE, tears welled in Beverly's eyes, and pins stabbed her chest. But as Darry turned the ornament so she could see the front, those tears fell away and something inside of her grew warm and toasty, like a fire meant to dry out wet winter stockings.

The shape of the ornament was now clear. It was a house.

A white house with a blue front door.

CHAPTER 45—QUINN

Quinn's house was the second stop on the circuit for the night. Harbor Hills merrymakers would come to 696 for appetizers. Likely, Quinn expected, they'd have hot cocoa with puffs of whipped cream on hand—or maybe apple ciders. Beverly was also serving mulled wine, and Quinn was anxious to get her hands on one of those. But first things first, she had to put the finishing touches on her and Vivi's outfits before the guys arrived.

Quinn invited Forrest, and Vivi invited Eli, of course. With the two-fold task of serving appetizers *and* passing out the town's special limited-edition Christmas stockings, it made sense to have a little extra help. Anyway, Quinn figured that night would be as good as any for Vivi to have a chance to bond with Forrest.

Not because she wanted to replace Vivi's father, no. And in fact, the whole issue of paternity had been the biggest obstacle preventing Quinn from arriving at tonight with emotional clarity. She'd gone back and forth and back and forth over whether to make an issue of the whole thing.

Confessing to her girlfriends had been a great start. She'd felt a weight lifted.

In the end, it was her daughter *and* her ex who'd helped Quinn see the snow-covered trees through the forest.

The day before, when Quinn was scrubbing the toilets and washing every last linen in the house, Matt had shown up unannounced with Vivi trailing behind him.

She hadn't expected Vivi. Not one bit. Vivi had pouted and demanded that she stay in Birch Harbor with her best friend, Mercy, for the whole of winter break. Normally, one would expect the parent in Matt's position to encourage such a coup. But Matt didn't. He'd marched his daughter up to her mother's door and demanded that they all work out whatever the problem was.

And the problem, in their case, was—

Quinn. Quinn, who'd been monitoring Vivi's hand-washing. Quinn, who'd been obsessively wiping down tables and chairs and vacuuming nooks and crannies that were so well hidden even dust mites couldn't get into them.

Quinn, who'd had to apologize—both to Matt and to Vivi.

And, finally, to herself.

It was then, with Matt and Vivi present and imploring Quinn to get *real* help for her problem, that she realized she could only get help if she came clean. She could only *be* clean if she *came clean*, really.

And so, with a deep breath and a stomachache and the compulsion to wash her hands, she'd spilled it all for them to hear. Matt had already known over half the story—that they'd both seen other people. Vivi had known none of it.

Quinn had expected her to experience shock. Maybe to act out. To scream and yell and run clear back to Birch Harbor for good.

And, in fact, Vivi had started to. She'd jolted up, her face flushed with anger. But Matt had tugged her back down. He'd entreated their daughter to hash it out then and there. To explore her anger, but *not* to run. Not to hide. To be present. Because if she wasn't— if she didn't handle it in that moment, then she'd have been no better than her mother.

Miraculously, Vivi had listened to Matt and remained, sitting and fidgeting as Quinn had apologized and explained herself as best she could. And, to his credit, Matt had chimed in, too, with his own explanation about how sometimes parents did things they regretted. That they were human, too, and it was okay to be imperfect.

Before he'd left, he'd given Vivi the choice—return to Birch Harbor and spend the break there with her old friends or stay in Harbor Hills and continue to work on her relationships there. Mercy wasn't going anywhere.

"Then neither am I," Vivi had agreed.

Now, here they were: Quinn and Vivi playfully competing for position in front of the full-length mirror in Vivi's room.

For the evening, Quinn had opted for an elegant cranberry-colored silk blouse. Over it, she'd pull on a faux-fur coat, something she'd found in the bowels of the hoard. It was a big black piece that had once belonged to Irma Carlson—in her better years, Jude had guessed, happy to hear that Quinn wanted it. Jude herself preferred not to wear fur.

Anyway, after a trip to a specialist dry cleaner in Pinconning, the fur had come out clean and fresh and exquisite. Quinn paired it with leather leggings and chic black snow boots, and she struck a wintry, dramatic look. And yet the outfit would be wholly functional for an evening of traipsing from one house to the next. Although, she would mostly stick around her house with Forrest, passing out hors d'oeuvres and the stockings, filled with locally popped and glazed caramel corn and a pair of cotton mittens. Adorable and oh-so-small-town.

The doorbell rang, and the two exchanged a look. It could be only one of two people, and now they jostled through the door and downstairs.

Sure enough, Forrest waited on the doorstep, a sprig of mistletoe in his hand. He blanched when he saw that Vivi was there, too. "I didn't know—"

"Vivi's staying for the holidays, after all," Quinn explained beneath a flush of her own. As she stammered to defuse the awkwardly flirtatious gesture, it was Vivi who surprised them both by gently pushing her mother through the doorway. "Go ahead. Maybe he's lucky number three."

Quinn glared at her daughter, but it was a shared secret. An inside joke. And instead of being angry, she could only smile at her daughter. Her nosey, too-smart girl who was now working alongside Quinn on the weekends at the paper, where she was learning the business of journalism from the inside rather than the outside.

CHAPTER 46—VIVI

A chaste peck later, Forrest was in the house and following Quinn to the kitchen to check that everything was ready.

Meanwhile, a second visitor had arrived at the front door. Elijah, with a poinsettia abloom in his arms and a bagged gift dangling from one hand. He lifted it up for Vivi to take, then placed the red-flowered plant on the side table. "It's nothing big," he said sheepishly.

Vivi beamed and rushed into his arms. She wasn't afraid to admit that half the reason she'd wanted to come back to Harbor Hills was for him. And if there was one thing Vivi was learning, it was just how good of a friend a boy could be. And how good of a *boyfriend* Eli was. She'd texted him the night before—as soon as she'd forgiven her mother and made her mind up— and here he was, ready for her. Waiting for her. Like a knight in shining armor. Vivi couldn't be too sure she believed in young love, but she could be sure of one thing. She cared very deeply about Eli.

Vivi pulled the tissue from the gift bag he'd brought to find an envelope within. Carefully, she opened it and removed a hand-penned certificate on cream cardstock. Frowning, she read it aloud. "Enjoy a special dinner and evening at Birch Harbor's storied Heirloom Inn. Good for two guests."

Her eyes grew wide, and her mouth fell open. "What? You...booked a room at my stepmom's bed-and-breakfast...for *us*?" It was the oddest and most romantic thing in the world. And Vivi *knew* her mother was going to say *N-O*. But before Vivi could protest, her mother and Forrest rejoined them in the front hall.

"It's okay. Eli talked to your dad and Kate. He'll stay in the attic rooms. You'll stay in your room there. Clara is going to chaperone." Clara, Vivi's half sister and other best friend besides Mercy.

"For real? We're like—going on a vacation together?" Vivi glowed above the certificate and fell into Eli's embrace. "This is so cool."

"Yeah, after Christmas."

"I hope my dad didn't make you *pay*." Vivi laughed.

Eli shrugged. "It's more of a gesture, I guess. And that's only half the gift, anyway."

"Half?" Vivi suppressed an even wider grin, playing it as cool as she could.

He nodded toward the gift bag, and while she pulled at another layer of tissue, Eli started in on an explanation. "I figure you needed one of your own. You know? Something that represented you and not just the house you live in?"

She pulled up a delicate silver chain, at the end of which hung a pendant the same size as the one she now wore—the one Jude had let her keep. This one, though, wasn't a *B*. It was a *V*. Vivi looked at Eli, nearly speechless, groping the air for the right reaction, the right words. He looked nervous, though, and rambled on.

"I mean I know your last name is Fiorillo, but your mom's is Whittle, and I wanted to respect both, you know? And like—feminism or whatever, so I went with—"

Before he could say another word, and despite the fact that her mother and her *boss*, Forrest, were watching, Vivi pressed her lips into Eli's and kissed him hard and good.

"I have a gift for you, too." After shopping and wrapping with her mom, Vivi had had another idea about something to give Eli. Something with a little more emotional value. She reached down below the hall table and picked up a gift bag of her own.

Mirroring her own unwrapping, Eli slowly plucked layers of tissue from the bag until he removed the frame. Inside of it, a picture.

She could see his eyes grow wet, and now it was Vivi's turn to explain. "I know how much you loved her. I got it from Beverly when she was packing the house. Kayla had it in her bedroom, I guess."

In a very small way, it hurt to give Eli a piece of another girl—and a *dead* girl, at that. But in a big way, it was the right thing to do. The *good* thing to do.

"Mrs. Castle?" Eli asked, his eyes never leaving the image of him and his deceased best friend hanging out in the cafeteria at school. "She gave you this?"

"Yeah," Vivi answered. Her mom and Forrest had left again, and it was now just the two of them, sharing a moment that was maybe too hard for young people. A moment that made them grow up a little bit. "But there's more," she added, praying she hadn't diluted the moment.

Eli wiped away a tear and set the frame down to reach back into the bag, removing a second framed photo. His sadness dissipated enough for them both to look at that second picture. One of them together in her home. The house on Apple Hill Lane.

CHAPTER 47—ANNETTE

Annette allowed Roman to pull her away from the parlor window and her blurry view into the front room of Quinn's house, where her son was giving his heart to another neighbor girl.

Elora and the babies were there, too, munching away on the main course, which Annette and Roman would be serving to guests who made their way from Beverly's house to Quinn's and then to hers.

In every way, Elora was beginning to turn into something of a daughter to Annette. It was nice to have a much younger friend—it was nice to have young children on the street again—and it was nice to make Elora go out for drinks on a Friday. Despite the young mom's protests, Annette insisted it was never too early to create *me* time. If there was one thing Annette was good at, in fact, it was the very idea of leisure activities for the parent set. And one day, Elora would want to meet a man again. One day, she'd be ready to move on from her philandering husband and nurture a healthy relationship.

But that time was far off, and for now, Annette enjoyed the socialization that a single friend offered. Besides, Roman had found out that Elora's parents were also in the *biz*. They did marketing for small businesses, and if there was one thing The House around the Corner Realty could always use, it was another infusion of PR. Especially after Annette had to step down from her role as a Realtor in their family business.

As for Roman and Annette, their marriage had never been better. With Eli veering closer and closer to college, it only made sense that Roman and Annette practice being a married couple again. What were they going to do when they became empty nesters? Sit around and stare at each other all day?

In the meantime, Annette had legal matters to attend to. Luckily, with a fierce attorney like Shamaine at her side—and with the support of Roman, a steadfast husband and best friend—handling the charges was manageable. Anyway, they were relatively light. Mainly, she'd been slapped with misdemeanor tampering charges. Those carried fines and community service. And she did lose her Realtor's license.

But Annette wasn't a quitter, and she had a great idea waiting in the wings. Very quickly, she came up with a plan for a second, smaller home business. She'd wait until Valentine's Day to roll it out, however, since that would be the most appropriate season for a debut.

A matchmaking service for small-town singles. If Annette could match people with the right home, she was positive she could match them with the right partner. And what was more, Annette had proof that she knew how to find true love. After all, she herself had found it. She'd found it, and she'd *kept* it.

All she needed for the business was a great name.

Now, as Annette and Roman stood together at their kitchen window, watching a troop of bundled-up locals tromp over from Quinn's house, their bellies primed, Roman snapped his fingers. "I've got it," he declared.

"Got what?" she asked, turning the Christmas music on in preparation to greet the gala-goers.

"Your business name."

"I'm all ears," Annette replied, smiling and leaning into her husband as he wrapped an arm around her shoulders.

"The Matchmaker around the Corner."

CHAPTER 48—JUDE

J ude stood in a cowl-neck flannel poncho at the edge of her property. Lately, as if she knew she needed it, Liebchen had taken to letting Jude carry her around. She stroked her cat now, and Liebchen purred.

A group of carolers following another small group of attendees turned the corner from Beverly's cottage and made their way toward Quinn's. That was five groups so far. One who'd just entered Annette's for their main dish. Now two at Quinn's for appetizers. And, according to their group text, two more groups who'd just arrived at Beverly's for drinks.

Of course, Jude's role in the whole thing wasn't in planning the logistics of the float from Beverly's to Quinn's to Annette's and then, finally, to Jude's house.

All Jude had been responsible for was to coordinate the dessert donations and decorate her house.

The latter, in fact, had been much harder. It was easy enough to enlist parish members to drop off cakes and pies, crumbles and cookies. But pulling out Christmas decorations and stringing them up was another matter. Jude had thought those days were long gone. The days of decorating for other people. Of celebrating holidays in that garish, outward way. The tinny pop Christmas songs and the decked tree and twinkling lights.

It was Dean who'd come by earlier in the week, fresh off a job in the UP, with a truck bed of ornaments and string lights. He said he was taking them to St. Vincent de Paul, but Jude had reasoned that she may as well make use of them. It took Dean no time at all to have her house dressed to the nines in greens and reds and silvers and golds.

Having his help was nice, too, while Jude sorted through the legal battle she'd be facing. Luckily, she had Shamaine to help with all of that. Also luckily, Michigan's statute of limitations had long expired on the majority of those offenses in which Jude may have been implicated. Mainly, she had to deal with a lot of paperwork related to having Tippy's body reinterred near her family. And then there was the relocation of all the other Carlson remains. But that was the best thing to do, in the spirit of a fresh start. A clean slate. And a safe place for people to live in Crabtree Court.

Jude had asked Shamaine if she could join her on a trip to Arizona once the whole thing was over. A change in scenery would do her good. Shamaine had agreed readily, promising they'd take off after the first of the year and telling Jude to pack her shorts—January in Arizona was nothing like January in Michigan.

Presently satisfied that she still had some minutes before any guests would arrive, Jude turned from the street and studied her own house. Brilliant white lights shone across her roofline and up the gables. Like something out of a made-for-TV movie, her front-yard pine trees were bedazzled with shimmering, oversize ornaments and thinner strings of white lights. A great, big green wreath hung on her door, glowing against the red paint. Picture perfect. All of it.

It occurred to Jude that never before in her life had she enjoyed such a seasonal display. Never before had she herself accomplished such grandeur. And surely, never had she enjoyed such an accomplishment from others. Not from her grandparents. Not from Gene. Maybe, if she thought really hard and squinted her eyes really tight, she could conjure such memories from way back in her youth. Before her parents died.

Yes.

She could.

Jude could picture her father, balancing on a wooden ladder, perching a homemade angel atop a skinny fir tree in their family room. She could picture her mother standing below and calling for a drumroll before she plugged in the string lights on the tree, washing their home in the warmth of those perfectly festive bulbs. Jude could remember how she felt those few precious holiday seasons she'd had with her family. She could remember thinking that Christmas really brought her home to life. She could remember the last Christmas, when her parents gave her that special memento of who she was and from whom she came. The *B* necklace. The same one she had officially passed on to Vivi, who seemed to appreciate the past more than Jude ever could.

Never again had she experienced all of that Christmas magic. Not with Nana and Grandad in those brief early years. Not at St. Mary's.

Nor had Jude experienced Christmas magic years later with Gene.

Not years on, when she learned of her grandfather's passing and accepted that he wasn't the grandfather she thought he was. That his death meant as much to her as her grandmother's death had meant to him. That a heart attack alone in his house was a sad thing, but the private, nearly secretive funeral was enough to get Jude through the guilt and the pain that coalesced anew with each holiday season.

That magic had been gone for some time, yes. But over the years—little did Jude know—she'd been rebuilding her spirit and the magic she'd once known. Rebuilding it for some moment that felt close. She'd rebuilt it at Mass every Sunday. In her prayers for her parents' and grandparents' souls. In her confession over the pain she'd played a party to. In the forgiveness she'd continually sought from Grandad and Nana and even Tippy beyond the grave. And the forgiveness she'd sought within herself, too.

The sound of tires crunching over snow tore her attention from her beautiful house. Her special guest had arrived.

The truck door slammed, and Jude carried Liebchen back into her house. Every time she walked back in, the ghost of the pony wall greeted her, and even now she almost went to set Liebchen on it. But it was long gone, thanks to Dean, and Liebchen would have to patter his way to his little bed in the front parlor while she went out to greet her special visitor.

But before Jude could even turn to go back out the front door, he was already there, a dessert perched on one hand and a very large, heavy-looking gift bag hanging from the other.

"Figured I'd bring it tonight. Wasn't sure what our plans were regarding Christmas Mass."

Jude let herself smile. A full-faced, toothy grin as she pushed the door all the way open to let Dean inside, where he first stopped to give her a kiss on the cheek, just below the mistletoe he'd insisted on hanging.

"I thought we agreed," Jude rebuked in singsong. "No presents!"

"It's hardly a Christmas present, Jude. And I don't expect anything in return. Well, that's a fib. I suppose I *hope* you'll enjoy it."

Jude took the dish from his right hand. "Store-bought?"

"Eh," he replied, a tad bashful, "my mother whipped it up. It's an apple crumble, whatever the heck that is."

Jude examined the golden-crusted sweet, savoring its soft scent. "Mmm. And your mom is on her way?"

Dean nodded. "She'll be making the rounds with my dad. I think mostly they're nosey about what their sons are up to." He laughed.

They had just moments now until the first batch of dessert-eaters arrived, and Jude couldn't help it. She was anxious to see what Dean thought she'd enjoy.

"Can I open it?"

"I want to caution you," he answered, looking serious. "It's a strange gift."

"Hmm." Jude eyed the bag, spying what looked like a twig with some greenery. A miniature Christmas tree? Odd, indeed. But then, wasn't Jude a touch odd? She said as much and gave him a squeeze on the arm. "I'm sure I'll enjoy it. Whatever strange thing it is."

"Well, it comes with an explanation," he went on as she started tugging wrinkled tissue from the bag and further inspecting the sparse foliage on what was definitely a tree. She pulled the whole thing out as Dean tugged the bag away. "I just—well, I just always figured it was a little odd that there aren't any apple trees on this street. Who named it, anyway?" He blushed bright red. "Sorry—I know. Your grandad. Well, I just wondered, maybe when his kin first broke ground, this place was an orchard or something." Dean hooked a finger in the direction of the front yard. "I got a whole slew of them. Marked down at the nursery uptown, just off of Main Street."

Jude frowned at him. "A slew of what?"

"Apple trees, a'course." Dean scratched his neck and gave a sheepish grin, shrugging and pinching one of the scrawny limbs. "It's a bare-root apple tree. Got a whole lot. Figured we could plant 'em in the front yard here. If you want to, I mean."

"Apple trees," Jude said on a whisper. "And apple crumble." It was...too perfect. Jude found herself overcome with emotion. With the thought of hosting over half the town in her house—the house that once belonged to her family. The house in which her grandmother had died. The one she'd *bought* from her grandfather. The house that she had made a home.

The house that didn't even feel like much of a home until now. Until this very Christmas season. Thanks to her friends. To Dean.

"You don't know what these mean to me," she murmured, her eyes on the fledgling fruit tree.

Dean's hand found its way to hers. "No. But I know what *you* mean to me. And a whole orchard of apple trees would never be enough to show you that, Jude. But I don't know how else. I don't know you. What makes you tick." He scratched his neck again. "You know at church how the priest talks about the mystery of our faith?"

She pressed her lips together and met his gaze, nodding yes. She did.

"That's how I feel about you, too, Jude. I haven't known you long. You're a mystery to me. But I believe there's something more. There could be a whole lot more. To us." He paused, and she could hear him swallow hard. "Do you believe that, too?"

Jude held his stare and again nodded. "Yes."

Liebchen interrupted them with a loud purr before anything could happen. Another touch. A kiss. He purred louder and pawed at the door.

Jude stilled, and so did Dean beside her. They could hear the group now, singing softly, a somber Christmas hymn—"O Holy Night." One of Jude's favorites. A holy night is exactly how it felt. Jude squeezed Dean's hand in hers. Then went for the door, where she could hear perfect strangers, neighbors, and other Harbor Hills residents—people who'd probably known Jude's ancestors, the Carlsons, without even knowing her. She could hear them admiring the house. Jude's house.

The house at the bottom nook of a hill on a street that would one day have apples, on Apple Hill Lane.

The house that Jude almost lost, but that—with her friends and her town—she saved.

The house that Christmas made.

～

THANK you for reading *Harbor Hills*. If you've enjoyed this saga, you might like to try *The Manger House*. Don't forget to join my newsletter to learn more about my books and me!

ALSO BY ELIZABETH BROMKE

Harbor Hills:

The House on Apple Hill Lane (1)

The House with the Blue Front Door (2)

The House around the Corner (3)

The House that Christmas Made (4)

Heirloom Island

Birch Harbor

Hickory Grove

Gull's Landing

Maplewood

ACKNOWLEDGMENTS

Big thanks to my fabulous team of editors. Elise Griffin, Beth Attwood, Tandy Oschadleus, you are so important to me! Thank you for all you do to make my stories shine. You are each invaluable to me.

Wilette Cruz, thank you for designing such gorgeous covers for Harbor Hills. You've brought to life Apple Hill Lane and this idyllic town. I wish I could live there thanks to your talented artwork. Just gorgeous. I'm so lucky to have you!

Every book I write, I write for my family. Especially my always-supportive Ed and my budding storyteller, Eddie. Love you boys. And the pups, too!

ABOUT THE AUTHOR

Elizabeth Bromke writes women's fiction and contemporary romance. She lives in the mountains of northern Arizona with her husband, son, and their sweet dogs, Winnie and Tuesday.

Learn more about the author by visiting her website at elizabethbromke.com.

Made in the USA
Middletown, DE
03 August 2023